10

D0887983

THE GILLESPIE COUNTY FAIR

THE
GILLESPIE
COUNTY
FAIR

A NOVEL

MARC HESS

GREENLEAF
BOOK GROUP PRESS

Published by Greenleaf Book Group Press
Austin, Texas
www.gbgpress.com

Distributed by Greenleaf Book Group

For ordering information or special discounts for bulk purchases, please contact Greenleaf Book Group at PO Box 91869, Austin, TX 78709, 512.891.6100.

Design and composition by Greenleaf Book
Cover design by Greenleaf Book Group
Cover images: ©Maverick C. Used under license from Shutterstock.com, ©Gordana Sermek. Used under license from Shutterstock.com, ©Chuck Wagner. Used under license from Shutterstock.com, ©Hank Shiffman. Used under license from Shutterstock.com, ©Fotoluminate LLC. Used under license from Shutterstock.com, ©Delcroix Romain. Used under license from Shutterstock.com, Back cover image: ©Jacqueline Cooper. Used under license from istockstock.com.
Author photo courtesy of White Oak Studio, Fredericksburg, Texas

Publisher's Cataloging-in-Publication data is available.

Print ISBN: 978-1-62634-604-8

eBook ISBN: 978-1-62634-605-5

Part of the Tree Neutral® program, which offsets the number of trees consumed in the production and printing of this book by taking proactive steps, such as planting trees in direct proportion to the number of trees used: www.treeneutral.com

Printed in the United States of America on acid-free paper

19 20 21 22 23 24   10 9 8 7 6 5 4 3 2 1

First Edition

*To Marc and Janet Bennett, who dragged
me down here against my will.*

For that I am eternally grateful.

Contents

ACKNOWLEDGMENTS

Writers of fiction spend an inordinate amount of time alone in their cave—inside their own heads—toiling to coax a complete world out of a blank sheet of paper. That is what it takes to get a good story. But writers need to pick up a few angels along the way in order to make that story into a book that can be shared with others. Steve Adams, my friend in letters and Writing Coach, taught me that. Without his persistent encouragement and critical perspective you would not be reading this.

My first developmental editor, Jo-Ann English, found a story in the mess of words that I showed to her and gave me a methodology for moving forward.

Throughout this writer's journey and throughout my life, Doug Stevenson has been my most enduring friend and the harshest critic of my work.

Jodi Egerton kept the wheels on when I thought I should be saving the entire world in the pages of this one book. "Stop that," she insisted. I did.

David Aretha, with Austin's Yellow Bird editors, and Donna Snow Robinson did the painstaking, nit-picky (or is it pernickety?) copy editing of this manuscript as it went through fourteen revisions.

It was my editor at Greenleaf, Amy Dorta McIlwaine, who helped baste the diction and flavor these words to make them taste really good.

More than anywhere else my depth as a writer grew through my long-time involvement with The Writers League of Texas—an invaluable resource for writers at all stages of their journey.

But most of all it was Lorrie, who lured me out onto the precipice with that wry smile of hers, brought her lips up to my wincing ear, and whispered, "Say Geronimo!"

An Enduring Heritage

There was no need to switch on the bathroom light. He knew where everything was, and besides, it wasn't his bladder that had him traipsing around in the dark. It was a different kind of rousing in his gut—a primal sense that something terrible was stirring.

He toed his way across the bedroom, where his wife lay snuggled in the sheets as if she were chilly. The nightstand clock told him that he could slip in beside her and catch another hour of sleep, but a blush of color flickering in the night sky lured him out onto the breezeless terrace instead. A bolt of adrenaline shot through his body before his mind registered what he was seeing.

In the town below, a fire billowed skyward like the blossom of some exotic flower: so rich and majestic that an entire neighborhood danced in its orange glow while its flames tongued a false dawn out of a black sky. Where, exactly, and how big? It was hard to guess from his hillside perch. Could be any one of those old stone workshops down along the creek. Whichever one it was, this would be an absolute disaster for one of the old families of Fredericksburg.

He threw on the bedroom lights, jolting his wife from her sleep as he crashed about, grabbing for his clothes.

"Fire. Down Lincoln Street. Near the creek. Where are my new boots?" He shot out of the room and then back in again. "It's a doozie, too. Someone's gonna be out a lot of building."

Cora Lynn sat up and pulled the retainer from her mouth. "Well, call the fire department."

"They're already there." He pushed his shirttail into his jeans while scanning the closet. There were probably six pairs of boots in there, but not the ones he wanted.

"So, what are *you* going to do? You're not a fireman."

He answered her with a shrug that fell somewhere between *Don't you get it?* and *I don't know.*

But she wasn't going to let it go. "You just let the fire department handle this, sugar."

On his way out the door, he called back to her. "You know it's going to be someone we know." Then, from further away: "Where the hell are my new ostrich-skin boots?"

"Honey!" she called after him, then fell back against her pillow. "Turn off the light."

He stuck his head back in the door. "Found 'em."

• • •

Heat singed the leaves on the old oak trees that lined Lincoln Street, where a rookie cop was rolling out yellow tape to block off the area. He walked right past the officer, mesmerized by the grandeur of it all, one hand holding the brim of his Resistol against the heat.

"Sorry, sir," the cop called out. "This is an active fire zone. You can't—"

"That's okay, son." He hurried by without making eye contact. "I'm Carel Geische."

The scorch of the blaze pressed against his body and warmed his cheeks. The fire trucks and all the grisly action were playing out on the far side of the one-lane bridge. Dissolving into the blazing crucible was the old Ortner Gingerbread Trim factory, where three generations of Ortners had cut and pieced frieze boards into a Bavarian-style latticework that used to be popular in the old cottages of Fredericksburg. This morning that material provided the ideal tinder for a Class A fire that would devour every timber, collapse every doorjamb, and melt away the wavy crown glass windows of the old mill. After this fire, even those fourteen-inch limestone block walls would be charred—but still standing.

What a perfect location, Carel thought. It was just far enough off Main Street to avoid the zoning restrictions of the Historic District and there was the quick access to the San Antonio highway—the perfect location for professional office suites built in the signature Geische, neo–Hill Country style: burnt limestone walls with rustic beams but none of that old gingerbread trim.

The greedy flames reflected in the plate glass windows of Ritzi Agricultural Equipment, the first shop across the bridge, where Carel's gaze found the plug-shaped Heinie Ortner standing with the willowy Jock Ritzi, two grown men who ran the enterprises their fathers had started on opposite sides of the creek. Carel approached them with the demeanor of a summons server—somber and erect. When he was within reach, Carel threw his arms around Heinie and took his old friend in a bear hug.

"Looks bad, Heinie. Real bad."

It was Jock who looked like he was on the brink of tears. "Look at that." He gestured with his chin as if none of them had seen the fire yet. "Looks to me like you're gonna lose it all. Everything."

Heinie was the calmer of the two—just standing there, his head bobbing up and down, responding to every sympathetic comment with some random biblical reference. "Everything has a purpose. We can't know His plan."

The three of them stood in a row, each one watching the fire from under the brim of his cowboy hat, dolefully going through a litany of what was lost.

"All those template-tables my pa and my *opa* made before I was even born," Heinie mumbled. "Gone. Can't be made again."

They shook their heads in unison.

"That old Kluge embossing press y'all hauled over from Germany," Jock remembered. "Probably the last one of its kind."

"Oh, we got that out a couple weeks ago," Heinie told them. "It's out in our barn now."

"What'd you go and do that for?" Jock asked.

"Oh, we're gonna fix it up. Sell it. It's worth some money, you know."

When the tallest of the flames could no longer reach over the top of the limestone walls, the first streaks of the true dawn lapped the horizon, absorbing the colors of the fire and promising another hot day across the Texas Hill Country.

Jock turned to their friend. "You've got this insured, right?"

"Sure thing. Yeah. I figure I'm gonna take away some seventy-three, eight hundred."

Carel slowly turned his eyes to the shorter of his two buddies, keen to catch the expression on Heinie's face when he answered the next question. "Seventy-three thousand, eight hundred dollars. That's a pretty precise number. How do you know that?"

Heinie thrust his hands down into the pockets of his Carhartt overalls, his head still bobbing under that black hat of his. "Well, we checked on that already. A bit ago."

"Un-huh," Carel acknowledged.

Jock nodded too. Then they all returned their stares to the slow-burning remnants of the millworks and stood in uneasy silence. In those coals Carel saw yet another small piece of his hometown that was gone forever.

Struggling with a reverence for the moment and an impatience welling up inside him, Carel broke into the awkward hush. "Hey, Jock. Can we use your office for a moment?"

"Sure."

The three men each put a hand to their hat as they ducked under a garage door to enter the Ritzis' workshop. Jock led them across the concrete floor in darkness and then flicked a light on to reveal a cramped office swollen with dented file cabinets and odd machine parts.

Carel sat down in the chair at the desk, which was divided into two messy parts by a fat-back computer monitor. Behind him, Jock went to a small window to switch on the air conditioner. Heinie had to wait until Jock came around and lifted a stack of file folders off the seat of another chair before he could sit too.

Carel removed his Resistol and placed it on the desk before him. "You got any coffee?"

"Sure," Jock responded, "I'll get y'all some," and he left the two of them alone in his office, letting the door shut behind him.

Carel put his elbows on the desk and leaned into Heinie's face. "If you listen to anything I say, old buddy . . ." He left a pause long enough for Heinie to realize that this was serious. "You got to listen to me now." He stared at Heinie until he was certain that he had his friend's full attention. "Don't you file that insurance claim."

Heinie furrowed his brow, anger welling up in his eyes. "That's no business of yours, Mr. Geische. I just lost everything I own. That money is going to get me paid off. Up and goin' again."

"They're going to figure out you torched your own place, and you won't get nothing but a stretch of time down in the Huntsville state pen."

"What are you talkin' about?" Heinie jumped to his feet, his fists clenched, ready to fight. "I didn't do nothin' like you're sayin'."

Carel held his palms up and softened his eyes. "I don't know anything, Heinie. And I wouldn't say anything if I did." He gestured, and Heinie sat back down. "And those guys down at the volunteer fire department aren't going to go looking for anything either."

"Ya don't think so?"

"*Macht nichts.* They're only going to talk about this one until the next one comes along. Then they'll just forget about it." Carel's eyes narrowed. "But before those insurance guys lay out one dime, they're going to find out how that fire got started."

Heinie's entire face dropped into his jowls. His breathing went shallow, almost panting, but his eyes never left Carel's.

"They're going to bring a special team up here from San Antonio. They'll shine around one of those blue lights on all the burnt marks." Carel swung his arm through the air to mimic how they might work it. "They'll have a fancy chemistry set that'll tell them everything: where it started, how fast it spread, how hot it got." He paused. "And what started it."

"Oh, *Scheiße*!" Heinie sank down in his chair, removed his hat, wiped his brow, and put the hat back on. "I didn't think they'd bring one of those things down here."

"I really don't know how all that works, but they probably can't do an investigation unless you file a claim."

"And I was really . . . really . . ."

"I know you were." They sat in heavy silence without making eye contact until Carel spoke up. "I might be able to help you out, buddy."

Heinie raised his eyes hopefully.

"What if I buy the property from you?"

"You mean . . .Won't that look kind of funky?"

"I would have to buy it from you before the fire."

Heinie's face screwed up in confusion.

"We'll have to backdate some documents. When was the last time you spoke to your insurance company?"

"Last week of July."

"Okay. I'll have to get it dated before that. It'll be a letter of intent to buy. With some cash money up front for earnest. Something to get you going for now." Carel could see that Heinie wasn't fully following how this plan might work, but the man was desperate for a way out. "Of course we'll have to settle on a value after the fire for a final sell price of, say . . ." Carel shrugged. "Twenty grand."

"Twenty grand!" shouted Heinie, coming out of his seat again. "I was going to get more than seventy-three from insurance."

Carel shook his head. "You were going to jail, buddy."

Heinie threw up his hands as though he could fight his way out of this trap. "*Gott verdammt!*" he shouted. After exhausting himself with air punches, he fell back into the chair and squirmed around for a bit.

When Heinie stopped his contortions at last, Carel stood and put his hat on, rounded the desk, and held out his hand— the time-honored way that old Fredericksburg families sealed their agreements.

Heinie gave him a bitter look but took his hand.

Carel held the handshake firmly. "I'll get the paperwork done. You'll just have to sign it all."

"I will, Carel. And I guess . . . I guess I should thank you. But damn it all."

"I know. This isn't what I wanted to happen, either. But I'm glad that I was here to help you out."

Jock kicked the door open with his boot, struggling as he clutched three Styrofoam cups steaming with coffee. "First pot. I had to get the water heated up and all."

Carel took one cup off Jock's hands. "Hard day, buddy." Carel gave Heinie a reassuring pat on the shoulder and walked out the door, calling back over his shoulder, "Thanks for the coffee, Jock."

• • •

Including its clock tower, the bank on the corner of Main and Llano was the tallest in a block of two-story buildings that stretched from the little shops wrapped around the Marktplatz all the way down to the old Nimitz Hotel, now a museum. One street: That was pretty much all there was to Fredericksburg, a small dot on a Texas road map that reminded visitors of a quaint hometown where they imagined that they would have liked to spend their childhood.

Outside the bank, a teller was setting out a board that advertised the Rate of the Day like a burger joint would announce the daily special. Carel grabbed the door before it closed behind her.

"Oh, Mr. Geische," the teller called after him. "You can't go in yet. The bank isn't open until—"

"That's okay, sweetheart. I'm here to see Mr. Schrubb."

Charles Schrubb, an old school chum, had inherited the bank president's position from his father back when it was called the Gillespie County Savings and Loan. Now he was the branch manager working for new owners in Houston. Carel crossed through his lobby, greeting several of the bank employees by their first names before swinging into Schrubb's office as if it were a public restroom.

Carel dropped himself into one of the deep leather chairs without so much as a glance at the deer head mounted on the wall above it. He cleared a spot on Schrubb's desk where he could set his Resistol. "I need about fifty grand. Short term."

"You are truly amazing, Carel." By his broad grin, Schrubb seemed amused by the request, but his tone was brusque. "Can you even grasp how overextended you are at this point in time? End of this month, the Loan Committee meets here, and one of our agenda items is 'Carel Geische, Foreclosure.' We have a whole agenda item devoted just to you, Carel." He paused, squinting across the desk. "We have already sent you a thirty-day demand letter. Didn't you get that?"

"Yeah, I got that." Carel shrugged it off. "And that's what I'm here to talk about. How to get you paid off. The sooner I can get this fifty, the sooner I can get back into the good graces of your illustrious financial institution."

"I don't want to hear it." Schrubb turned his attention to something that had popped up on his computer monitor.

"I'm making good on a letter of intent to buy the Ortner Gingerbread Trim shop."

Schrubb shot up like a jack-in-the-box. "The one that's still on fire! You are unbelievable, Carel." He leaned forward and pushed a button on his desk phone. "Beverly. Are you there? I have Carel Geische in my office. You have to hear this. And I need a witness. Bring a tape recorder."

Beverly had become the senior loan officer when Schrubb became branch manager—she moved up when he went down. She stepped into the room now with a tin smile and a dry "Good morning, Carel."

"Bev." He nodded. They had dated once. Just once.

Neither offered a handshake, but Carel scooted to the other chair, offering her the seat next to him. Beverly, however—a little overdressed for mid-August in South Texas—preferred to stand, probably to keep the wrinkles out of her crisp business suit.

"This is about the Ortner family, who just lost everything they ever worked for." Carel put on his best puppy-dog face. "A while ago I signed an LOI with Heinie. To buy the land under his shop. Now, after what happened this morning, I just can't go back on it."

Beverly was studying him with an acrimonious look that reminded Carel of the end of that one date. Carel turned to Schrubb. "We graduated high school with him. You dated his sister."

"His cousin." Schrubb was quick to set the record straight. "And that was just for one football season. We just went out so she could see his games."

Carel waved away Schrubb's comment. "The Ortners have been family here since forever. When this was your daddy's bank, it took care of the families who founded this town."

"That's why it's not my daddy's bank anymore." Schrubb filled his cheeks with air and let it out slowly as he leaned back in his creaky leather chair. "This is not the bank it used to be. Our loans are underwritten in Houston now."

Carel leaned in. "It's not about the money, Chuckie."

Schrubb winced at Carel's use of his grade-school nickname.

"This is about who we are and whose side you're on," Carel continued. "Are we really going to sell out the founding fathers of Fredericksburg for some quick tourist dollars?"

"It's not like that at all, Carel." Schrubb gestured to a neat stack of file folders on his desk. "We're the local bank. Most of our loan dollars go right back into this community."

"That's what your Houston-printed brochures say, but look at 'em." Carel reached across the desk, almost touching the file folders on his desk. "Any local family names on that big stack of approved loans? Or is it all just tax write-offs and hobby wineries for the rich yuppies who come down here and don't really cotton to the gritty side of quaint. While we,"—he pounded his chest—"the families that built this town, are going extinct."

Carel caught Beverly trying to disguise her smirk by turning her attention to the customers meandering into the lobby now that the bank was open for business.

Schrubb leaned across his desk, looking Carel in the eye. "Not that we're going to put up any money, Carel, but just out of curiosity, what were you going to do with Ortner's place?"

"Historical restoration!" Carel's arms flew into the air. "I am doing what I can to hang on to our way of life."

Schrubb was shaking his head. "Noble causes don't make good investments, Carel. It's a—"

Before Schrubb could finish, Carel's phone rang. He stood and drew it from his holster, quick as a six-gun, then flicked it open while pointing a finger at Schrubb. "That's Houston talking, *alter Freund*." Then, into his phone: "What?"

Beverly looked at her watch, then stepped right up into Carel's face. "Take your call outside. We conduct bank business here."

Carel covered his phone with his hand. "Excuse me, Bev, but it was *you* who busted into *my* meeting."

"You're not *in* a meeting," she hissed up at him. "You're talking on your phone."

Ignoring her, Carel returned to his call, louder than before. "They're a bunch of old Krauts, for God's sake. You don't get paid to speak to the Historical Society. You get paid to pound nails. Remember that!"

Schrubb spoke up from behind his desk. "I have to get to work here." He flapped his hands in shooing gestures directed at Carel, who re-holstered his cell phone and picked his hat up off the desk.

"I gotta run, buddy. I got some ass to kick." He pointed down at Schrubb. "But you need to do me right. Don't talk to Houston. You make the decisions right here in Gillespie County, just like your daddy did. Fifty grand." As he stormed out of the office, his voice rose loud enough for the whole lobby to hear. "I have to go do battle with the *Gott verdammt* Historical Society."

Carel's confidence fell to the floor when he saw her standing at a teller's window, one of the first bank customers that morning, turning just in time to catch the drama rolling out of the branch manager's office. His daughter.

He took a breath to stave off the swell of nausea that accompanied these surprise encounters with her, these random ambushes that happened again and again over so many years: picking out vegetables at the Farmers Market, riding her bicycle down Austin Street, in the congregation at a cousin's wedding. He should be used to it by now—watching her grow up, but having no hand in raising her . . .

Carel took a moment to quell the tightening knot in his

stomach before approaching her with a casual greeting. "So, *wie gehts*, Willow?"

"Hi, Dad." She spoke in a quiet tone, maybe even embarrassed.

Just *Hi, Dad*—that was the next pang to hit Carel. *Hi, Dad*, as if everything was all right with them. As if these weren't the first words she'd spoken to him since she graduated high school two years ago.

Carel argued, to all who would listen, that he had made an effort to fit into her life: He'd given her his old work truck. He'd remembered her birthday most of the time. And he'd hoped that the success of his business, his enhanced stature in town, would somehow bring her running back to him, at least when she grew up and needed a job. But Willow didn't seem impressed with any of this. Now here she was, at the bank and looking all grown up, and he didn't really know her at all. That pauperized him.

He didn't fancy that piece of jewelry she had stuck in her nose, but he tried not to let on to that, either. Other than that, she looked like every other unmarried girl in town, with a billowy blouse, denim shorts (way *too* short), and her mom's jet-black hair intentionally falling in her face, like she wanted everyone to know she'd just gotten out of bed. There were no tattoos—that he could see.

"So, what are you up to?"

"Gettin' change," she answered. "Me and Mom, we got this yard sale comin' up. What you been doin'?"

"Just . . . fixing some history."

She shrugged approvingly. "Cool," she said, but the blank look in her eyes told Carel that she didn't know what he was talking about.

"Did you walk down here? Need a ride?"

"Nah. I got the truck." She hesitated and put out a coy smile. "I mean . . . yeah. The truck you gave me."

"That old starter solenoid still holding up? It used to give me problems."

"Yeah. It's all running real good."

"That part is bound to go out on you one day. When it does, let me know. I'll fix it for you. I could write it off as a business expense." He paused, but Willow gave no response. "You know, I drove that truck a long time. It's a good one."

"Been good to us, too. But yeah, okay. Thanks. We'll take ya up on that."

"Anything I can do to help you with your yard sale? I have a lot of expensive stuff I could throw in. You could keep the money."

"What we got is *too much* stuff. That's why we're havin' a friggin' yard sale."

Carel bristled at the profanity. *Her mother's mouth,* he thought. *I could have fixed that.*

"Okay, then." He nodded in acceptance. "You call me if you need anything, *liebling.*"

Willow pushed a deferential smile toward him and returned her attention to the teller. Carel slipped out the bank door, having reached the full extent of his parenting.

• • •

To get that old truck started, Willow had to lean on the key four or five times. It had been going on like that for a while, and her mom fussed at her about not tromping on the gas while she was cranking it. "Wouldn't help," her mom would say. "Got nothin' to do with the gas. It's a bad starter." Eventually the solenoid would catch and the old Ford Super Duty would roar to life. It was a pain in the ass, but Willow wasn't going to ask Mr. Carel Geische to fix it for her. As far as she was concerned, she'd settled with him a long time ago.

In Fredericksburg it was hard for a child to tell, exactly, when it was that her father had left. He'd keep coming around on weekends for a while. He'd show up at occasional family gatherings. And then she'd be seeing him around town for the rest of her life, like just now at the bank. But Willow knew exactly when she had been done with him.

It was in the summer before her fourteenth birthday, late one night, alone in her bedroom up on the second floor of an empty house. She'd been sitting on the floor cross-legged, wearing only panties and a large T-shirt, a razor blade in her hand. And she'd felt no trepidation or sense of wickedness the first time she'd pushed that rapier into her thigh.

Bending over her legs, the same way she folded herself to paint her toenails, Willow had pressed the keen tip against the softest part of her leg. At first it just pushed the skin down, making a dimple but not breaking through the surface.

What's with this? were the words that scrolled through her mind.

Bravely she'd increased the pressure, fighting off an instinct to pull her hand away, until the tip of the razor broke through the surface and the pliable flesh rose up on either side of the blade to take the thin blue steel into her body. She had paused with the tip sticking in her just the tiniest bit, waiting for the pain. It didn't hurt, really, and there was not much blood at all.

"That's weird," she'd whispered to herself.

Carefully, she had drawn the scalpel through the surface of her skin, as smooth as the pull of a zipper, all the way up to the elastic band of her underwear. Flesh had fallen open on either side of the cut, looking something like a slice made in a marsh-mallow. It wasn't messy at all.

Now what?

Her second laceration, slow and deliberate like the first, went just a tad deeper and ran around the circumference of her thigh, intersecting the first cut at a right angle. This cut, too, was trailed by a tiny furrow of white flesh that slowly filled with a line of her own blood. Willow had given this cut a name.

"Llano Street," she'd declared aloud.

Naming that cut meant that her first stroke was Main Street. With two streets named, Willow had gotten her mind around the pattern she would carve into herself. The next cut, a slice that wasn't quite straight, was Travis Street. Another quick slash made Washington Street. At this point, blood was seeping out of the earlier lines.

"Shit. Shit. Shit!" a more rational voice had cried through her clenched teeth. Willow had used the tail of her T-shirt to dab at the little crimson drips. Not a lot of blood, but she'd known those stains would be hard to get out, and she didn't want anyone to know.

On the inside of her left thigh had appeared a blood-scrawled street map of the route her father had driven to drop her off at home earlier that night. She had leaned in to make one last cut, a small and haphazard *x* to mark the spot where she was right then, on Washington Street: her safe house, her place in the world.

She didn't want to see him anymore, and she had told him so. He'd insisted that they go out for brats and currywurst on his visitation day—the one day that the Gillespie County divorce court made fathers visit the children they had walked out on. She hated it. It was like he was supposed to be her babysitter, taking her out every other Wednesday so her mom could go out drinking with her friends.

"I'm old enough to be home alone, you know." Willow dropped the hint as they sat across from each other at Friedhelm's Bavarian deli, out where Main Street forked off to the west.

Her dad did the worst thing a parent could do: He didn't get mad. He didn't lecture her. He just let her words sail right over his head. "Come on now. You love brats and currywurst. Right, *liebling?*"

Willow hated that old German nickname. He had branded her with it when she was a toddler. *Can't you see I am not your* liebling *anymore?* But she couldn't bring herself to be mean to him out loud.

Her father had one of his everything-is-all-right kind of smiles hung across his face as he leaned across the plate of German fast food he had ordered for them to share. "I was a teenager too, you know," he said. "I understand how you feel."

No, you don't! she didn't say. Willow sat paralyzed, biting into her lip, hoping that a waitress would come over, or that her father would just give it up, or that the whole deli would explode in one great ball of flames. But none of those things happened.

"I don't want to do this anymore." The words just kind of tumbled out of her mouth. She had wanted to say that to him for a long, long time. She had waited her entire life to get revenge on him for leaving her and her mom, for leaving them poor and her mom pissed off all the time. So often she had imagined how great it would feel when she finally got to tell him off—but now, with it out, it didn't feel so good. Talking just made her feel worse.

Without raising her head, Willow peered up and saw his face flushed with indifference. He went on talking, but Willow was already gone. The only time she gave him a response was when he said, at long last, "Do you want to take the rest of this currywurst home with you?"

Willow shook her head. *No.*

"Sure you'll be okay home alone?"

She nodded eagerly. *Please get me out of here.*

Later, alone in her bedroom, Willow had breathed in the sense of relief that accompanied the numbing sensation, that drifted through her body while the blood on her thigh coagulated along its designated streets. The few places where tiny red rivulets crept down her leg had given her a palatable tickle, like a breeze blowing hair around her sweaty neck, before leaving tiny drops on the rug. Lying back on the floor, Willow had felt better then, much better—ebbing on an aberration of light warm air and letting her thoughts flow to other places, other times, days long ago when she was, indeed, her daddy's little *liebling.*

• • •

The stone house at the very end of Washington Street, where the countryside broke upon the town, was the only place Willow had ever lived. Her mom, too, had spent her entire life within these venerable walls that Willow's *opa* had built long before either of them were born. From the side facing other houses along the street, this gnarled slice of the Texas Hill Country looked like all the other old German farmsteads in Gillespie County: solid and practical, with a knot of outbuildings hidden from the street by five short rows of freestone peach trees. On the backside of the house, a treeless pasture fell away from a long wooden porch and rolled easily under the occasional hooves of black-headed Dorpers, all the way to the rocky bottom of Palo Alto Creek, where the barefoot days of so many summers had slipped carelessly through the tender fingers of Willow's childhood.

Fredericksburg itself endured as a rock-rimmed town of country-wide streets joining each other at precise right angles and held in place by tidy buildings made from limestone blocks. Many of the round and pleasant people who greeted each other in their singsong, German-English dialect were related in one way or another. It was hard for a kid to get in trouble in a community so intact. Willow couldn't ride her bike down Main Street without running into one of her cousins, her pastor, a teacher, or a friend of her mother. All these people would smile and look right through her, each of them seeming to know more about who she was than she did.

The worst day of Willow's life came somewhere near the end of her first year in high school, and it was her own fault. She found out how really stupid it was to start cutting on her arms. Of course her mom was going to find out sooner or later, and maybe that's what Willow really wanted. Her mom did find out, and after a tantrum to beat all, she dragged Willow off to have a talk with their pastor, where she pulled up Willow's shirt sleeve right in front of Father Huschmann. Laid bare in front of the poor bewildered pastor, she might as well have just shown him her nipples.

The cut marks above her elbow bore the indisputable evidence of her sins. Willow was sure she was going to descend into hell right there on that spot. Father Huschmann would pull a lever, and she would fall though some trap door. Or flamethrowers would light up and fry her, right in front of the crucifix that the nervous man twisted in his fingers while her frantic mother raged. But the more her mother ranted and the more Willow cried, the more obvious it became that Father Huschmann didn't have a clue what to do. He just told them to pray on it.

"Seek the guidance of our Lord," he said. If anything, he sort of laid the blame on Willow's mom when he said that "a broken family is the Devil's open door."

Willow was well aware that her mom had enough problems and didn't need this one. Soon after the inquisition with Father Huschmann, the short attention span of Willow's mother was hijacked by yet another crisis: Their water heater went out, right at the time that the property taxes came due. And Willow had gotten off scot-free with something that should have been the absolute end of her.

The other worst day in Willow's life came a year later, in the spring of her sophomore year, when she had to go to her dad's wedding. It was a big show-off church affair with a catered reception at Turner Halle. His new wife—Willow's new stepmom—smacked of dressed-up trailer trash, with makeup thicker than the icing on the wedding cake. Two new step-brothers, Justin and Jordan, were thrown into the deal as well. They would be living in her dad's big new house up on the hill. Willow went through the rest of her high school years watching her dad get richer and her mom get more overwhelmed by the common burdens of single motherhood.

As Willow heard it, her dad made his money first by selling off pieces of his family's land and building fancy houses on them, and then by fixing up stores in town to make them appear old-fashioned. The tourists were attracted to that old-timey look. Carel Geische got to be a big man in town who liked to throw his weight around and brag about his pioneer family name—which was also Willow's name. But Willow didn't see him as the Saint of Historical Renovation that he made himself out to be. The simple story was that he got rich buying and selling something that really wasn't his: the very history of Gillespie County.

• • •

A crew of Carel Geische's contract laborers were stranded on the roof of the Austin Street Bed & Breakfast. They were afraid to come down. Holding them at bay up there was a three-man delegation from the Historical Society, who stood on the front lawn waving papers at the workers and insisting they put their hammers down. The men on the lawn shouted at the workers in German. The roofers called back in Spanish. Matters got worse when Carel arrived at the building site after his run-in at the bank, running his truck up onto the lawn and scattering the docents from the Historical Society.

The folks from the Historical Society were threatening to get a restraining order that would require Carel to change his roofing plan to be more consistent with the traditional look of the neighborhood. Carel dismissed their suggestions by out-shouting them and running them off the property.

It wasn't until the hottest part of the afternoon that he found his way back to the air-conditioned offices of Geische Land & Development: Real Estate. "You guys sell anything today?" he shouted out to announce his entrance. It was his habitual greeting.

Two, three years ago, their firm had half a dozen licensed agents filling the desks in the front office. Now there were two: a retired Air Force officer who ran a ranch-load of Boer goats out on the Old San Antonio highway, and a cute young go-getter with a long string of bad luck in each and every aspect of her life. Carel's wife, Cora Lynn, held the broker's license for the firm and was the only one of them who had been to a closing in the past four months.

In the office Cora Lynn was a busy worker, deliberate with her paperwork and direct in her manner. At home she spent her evenings drinking margaritas and watching old John Wayne movies. She dressed with a cliché Texas flair that complemented Carel's contemporary cowboy style, and overall she came off as a gal who might have grown up as a rodeo girl—which she hadn't.

"I've got some papers for you to notarize," he said as he breezed past, continuing into his office, where he parked himself behind his desk.

All too familiar with his methods, Cora Lynn made him wait a while before she showed up at his door with her record book and stamp pad. "Do I need to fetch a witness for this?"

"Oh, no. I haven't even written up the papers yet. Going to be tricky. Do you just happen to have an empty line in that book—say, three, four weeks ago?"

She stepped forward and half-sat on the corner of his desk. "What are you up to, sugar boots? I heard you was at the bank this morning."

"Oh, I'm just buying some distressed property." He gave her a sly wink. "But we're buying it before it became distressed. Should be able to turn it in just a few weeks—after the smoke clears, so to speak."

"You just might be fixin' to get my notary's license revoked." She stepped up to him. "I love you, but I ain't going to jail for you."

"You already took a chance on me one time." Carel pulled her onto his lap. "You're not willing to risk another go?"

"Hell, no. If I go to prison, you can get an automatic divorce. Then you'll be running off with little Miss Go-getter out there."

He tried to lay a kiss on her, but she pushed him off.

"Other than that, there won't be no call for me to be notarizing your made-up papers. Bank's not going to be giving you any money, after all the damage you already done 'em." She stood up and straightened her clothes.

"You need to get yourself a more positive outlook, darling."

"You're a dreamer, Carel Geische." She walked to the door, turned back to him, and blew him a kiss. "And that's the part of you I'm in love with."

• • •

A couple of hours behind his desk made Carel antsy. The only things he did in the office these days were wrestle with unpaid bills and field calls from collection agencies. The only time he felt he was getting anything done was when he was out and about in his truck.

The doors of Carel's Ford F-450 Super Duty were emblazoned with his new company logo: a rustic lone star surrounded with the words *Geische Land & Development: Real Estate*. A heavy-duty work truck, it was a definitive part of Carel's identity. On Tuesday evenings that truck was always parked out at the softball fields, where he served as a volunteer umpire for the Fredericksburg Optimists' T-ball League. This allowed him to cozy up to the two county commissioners who sponsored the league—"two of the grumpiest 'optimists' I know," his wife had once told him—but important allies to have when Carel applied for building code variances.

When the evening games ended, Carel could count on returning home to find his wife on the south-facing patio—a double-shot margarita cooling her hand—watching the lights rise up from the little houses of Fredericksburg as the last long streaks of a slow red sun finally yielded their hold on the day.

He knew how Cora Lynn looked down upon Fredericksburg, the town where she, her mama, and her grandmama had all been raised, and raised poor in a double-wide trailer house just a whiff away from the county landfill. Carel was proud to have a girl as pretty as her take his name and work so eagerly alongside him. Years ago, amid a summer sunset not unlike this one, Carel had brought her out onto this same patio, when it was unfinished and owned by someone else. With one strong arm reining her up against his side, the other arm sweeping across the panorama below, he had said to her, "Someday, darlin', we are going to own this whole damn town." With those words he'd won her heart.

But tonight as he kicked off his boots in the front foyer, where he had found them that morning, it was, "Hey, sweet darlin'. Sell anything today?"

His wife came to him. "Not today, sugar boots. That contract down on White Oak still won't sign." She stood up on her tippy-toes to peck his cheek as he flipped through the mail.

"What's the damn holdup?" he bleated.

"The appraised value. Our bank found it a little out of kilter with the dumpy way the place really looks." She spoke over her shoulder as she headed to the bar to fetch him a drink and refresh her own, paying no attention to his mumbled response.

"*Our* bank is the one that's out of kilter."

Carel crossed through a corner of the too-spacious living room and threw some new envelopes onto a pile of papers that he was ignoring. Then he strode on down to the bedroom, where he took off his modern-day gun belt: cell phone, pager, buck knife, and all. "The boys coming for dinner?" he shouted back down the hall.

"Jordan's already been," Cora Lynn hollered back. "Just stopped by to clean up. He's taking that Keubel girl out to dinner at Friedhelm's."

"What? He just came by to steal my condoms, didn't he?" Carel ducked into his bathroom to check.

When he reemerged, Cora Lynn was in the bedroom doorway with his drink and a smirk. "Well, that would be a good thing, wouldn't it? Must have had a darn good mama, teaching him about safe sex and all."

Carel was used to losing arguments with her before they even started. As he took his drink, the phone on the nightstand started to ring.

Cora Lynn turned to get it, saying, "You wash yourself up, now. Dinner is just about on the table." She picked up the phone, exchanged the familiar pleasantries with someone, and passed the call to Carel.

"*Wie gehts*, Chuckie? You're working late. Got some good news for me?"

Cora Lynn left Carel to his conversation, which quickly lost its civility.

"No! You listen to me, buddy. You've got to grow some *cajones* and tell those sons of bitches down in Houston . . ."

When Carel rejoined his wife in the kitchen, he was perfectly calm and collected. "You were right about the bank. They got no more money to lend to me. Guess you get to stay an honest notary public for just a while longer."

She lay her hand on his forearm. "Don't you go frettin' about this one deal, sugar boots. We got each other. And we got this house."

Geische Manor was what Cora Lynn's two boys, Justin and Jordan, called it. They had been raised in that house from the time their mother had taken on the Geische name. Carel had built it in a neo–Hill Country style, using exposed limestone and rustic timbers that were meant to be reminiscent of the German pioneers. Rustic styling, yes, but far too elegant for a working homestead, with its sweeping atriums, floor-to-ceiling windows, and granite countertops. This had become the signature style of Geische Land & Development: Real Estate—lavish with a traditional bent. It was difficult to keep clean and spoke greatly of the affluence of the owner.

Carel had built the home, but not for himself. Years ago he was the contract builder for a Midland oilman who was squandering himself into bankruptcy during the construction process. Back in the early days of the real estate boom, the name on the side of his truck was *Geische Custom Framing— Construction*. Carel was the one who dug out the trench lines, drove the nails, and held the builder's lien. Filing for bankruptcy in Texas is, by design, a long, drawn-out process, and Carel used that time to expand the original house plans and add the inside-outside patio, the pool, and the hot tub—all on his customer's tab. When the bankruptcy court finally settled, Carel leveraged his builder's lien and a relatively small amount of cash for full ownership of the property. It was a clever way for a one-truck builder to move himself into such a grandiose property, which also brought him a big chunk of instant equity.

Carel could now sit at the dining table under the cypress pergola on the outside portion of his patio and look down across the open creek bottoms and onto the town proper. From there he could watch the setting sun glistening off the tin roof of the old German rock house at the end of the last street coming out of town, where the yellow field rose from the creek bed to the back door—the home of his first wife, Mari Hilss Geische, and their daughter.

That little house on Washington Street was a sore point between him and Cora Lynn because Carel got title to that property when he was married to Mari. In spite of Cora Lynn's

persistent suggestions, Carel remained bull-headed in his determination not to sell off any part of that property—at least while
Willow still lived there. Actually, it was more complicated than
that because Carel had, a long time before Cora Lynn came
into his life, put up his interest in Mari's house as collateral
for one of his first big business loans, and that particular note
was part of the package of debts that Carel's buddies at the
bank were now threatening to call in. Cora Lynn knew nothing
about that.

"Your sister called," came Cora Lynn's voice, jumping
into his distracted moment. "She's coming up this weekend.
Bringing her little girl, for the fair. I invited her to stay up here
with us, but she's made other plans."

"What's she doing with her kid? We're not getting stuck
watching her, are we?"

"Caitlin's gonna spend some time with her father."

"Dean?" Carel damn-near spilled his drink. "Jeanie's letting
my niece stay with that son of a wetback? He owes me money,
you know."

"We all know that, sugar boots. But Dean is her father.
Jeanie says that good or bad, Caitlin needs to get to know him.
That's her decision, and I agree with her. And if you can't offer
up a smile for that, you should just keep that down-in-the-
mouth look of yours all to yourself."

Carel settled into a rush of tequila and lime juice. "All that
little girl got from Dean Calderon was a Mexican name and
those thieving eyes. So, what's he going to do with my niece?
Take her out to some honky-tonk, feed her Jell-O shots, and let
his buddies grab at her ass? I'll have to put an end to that shit."

Another phone call put an end to their patio dinner. Carel
took it in his downstairs study. It was the attorney for the
Historical Society, calling with an official complaint about the

manner in which Carel had physically threatened representatives from the—

Carel hung up. He stayed in the study, scowling into his computer monitor, until Cora Lynn, now in a thin chemise, crept down the stairs to find him.

"It's time to give it a rest, sugar boots," she purred.

His hands moved from the keyboard onto her hips. As she ran a couple of suggestive fingers up to his shoulder, her mouth came close enough to his ear to take a bite. "And I got just what you need."

"Oh yeah?" He slid a hand under her gown. "And just what would that be, sweet darlin'?"

She held out a vintage video box—something, she told him, that she'd found on eBay. *Comanche Station,* the old Randolph Scott Western. In black and white. With that she lured him back upstairs, where she threw some popcorn in the microwave and served up the last of the margaritas. They sank together into the folds of their faux leather sofa under the glow of the forty-five-inch plasma TV screen mounted above the fireplace. Carel was snoring before old Randolph Scott could get word to the fort that the Comanche were on the warpath.

• • •

Too hot to sleep, too buzzed to lie still, Carel slipped out of the bed he didn't remember getting into. He pulled on a pair of boxers, stumbled through the dark into the kitchen, and poured what was left of the tequila straight into the nearest glass. Back downstairs, sitting in front of his computer, he tried once more to get different results from the same set of numbers.

The "study" itself had been an afterthought. The room was too big to be the wine cellar in the original house plans, and now it was filled with his stuff—a room that every young boy imagines for himself. One wall was dominated by an original G. Harvey print—cowboys in the rain—framed in mesquite, signed, numbered, and properly lit. It was a prize he had taken home from a Gillespie County Fair and Festival Association scholarship auction. On either side of the print hung the racks of deer he'd killed and the oak gun cabinet with his collection of Western firearms. Hogging up most of the space in the room was a pool table; shoved too close to the wall to be playable, it was covered with a white cotton drop cloth.

Carel rang up his sister, thinking he might just catch the Austin party girl at this late hour. He intended to bitch her out, once again, about Dean Calderon, but all he got was a recorded message.

It wasn't enough that Dean had gotten his sister pregnant. Their short marriage had then become the favorite topic for the family quarrels, which ended up driving Jeanie to take her baby and move off to Austin. Carel's affection for his little sister was genuine. They were the two youngest out of five kids on a ranch that was always struggling to make ends meet. While the rest of the Geische clan had moved past the catastrophe of her marriage, accepted her divorce, and gone back to their ranching, Carel never got over her leaving town—he just missed having his sister around. In his way of thinking, it was proper for the man to remove himself. But Dean Calderon wasn't German, and he stayed on to prey on other women, most recently Carel's own ex-wife. Dean was a pest who just needed to be shot—that's all there was to it.

Carel left a message on his sister's answering machine in the kindest tone, inviting her to bring her daughter up and stay with them at Geische Manor. His message ended, "Love you. Look forward to seeing you and, uh, Caitlin."

That done, Carel looked down at all the unresolved issues on his desk, took a long, slow sip of tequila, and stood up to shake it off. He picked up the old black-and-white photo of his uncle Victor and him leaning against a fence line at the Gillespie County Fair. *How long ago had that been, then?* Carel wondered. He looked maybe ten or eleven years old, standing on the bottom rail to make him look much taller than he was at the time.

Big hats and big smiles—it was a dark and grainy picture, but it was the one that Carel put into a frame after his bachelor uncle died—the image Carel chose to remember him by, with both of them wearing those big oval belt buckles. Victor had won many of those trophy buckles as a rough stock rider at rodeos and county fairs throughout the Hill Country and all of Texas. He had given one to Carel not too long before that picture was taken. The impressionable young cowboy relished it as if he had been given the entire history of Texas, and there was nothing grittier, nothing grander than all of that.

Some folks, including many in Carel's own family, talked about Uncle Victor drinking himself to death, but he didn't really die that way. Sure, Victor kept himself pickled a lot. He even tutored young Carel on how to handle his liquor—and on how to be a real Texan: "Ya don't back up, and ya don't back down."

Victor wasn't one to rot away with cirrhosis of the liver, becoming a burden to his family or disappearing into a nursing home. He was a lot more cowboy than that. Victor had stood up in the bed of a pickup truck one night when some of his buddies were delivering him home from a honky-tonk called the South Star, out on the San Antonio highway. Sure, he was drunk, probably had no idea where he was. Just stood up looking for a place to pee, and stepped out over the tailgate as the pickup raced down Tivydale Road, and that was all she wrote.

Rundown and way off the beaten path, Victor's hardscrabble ranch was more expense than equity. It passed to family hands, and Carel was one of those listed as a co-owner—a piece of real estate that figured large in his future plans.

Carel set the old photo back on his desk and meandered over to admire the toys in his gun cabinet. Collector's items, really. No one had much use for guns these days. You couldn't shoot bad guys anymore, and you needed jet fighters and nuclear warheads to defend the American way. Still, Carel was particularly fond of his matched pair of Italian replica 1872 US Cavalry revolvers, sporting seven-and-a-half-inch blue steel barrels and solid bone grips. They shot real .45-caliber bullets. He had a hand-tooled leather holster belt made so that he could wear them to the cowboy shooting reenactments he used to attend.

Naked except for his skivvies, Carel slipped the gun belt around his waist and dropped the pistols into the holsters. Emboldened by his armaments, he strode across the room for his Resistol. He was now pumped to the man of action that he reckoned himself to be, ready to take on bandits, Indians, and the whole damn Gillespie County Historical Society.

Sauntering up to the pool table, Carel took the corner of the white sheet in his hand and pulled it away with one swift jerk, the way a dining room magician would. And there lay his entire future: a scale model of the Ranger Creek subdivision, a protruding set of figurines spread out like a tabletop railroad town. It was a detailed architectural relief plat of the development that was going to emerge from Uncle Victor's ranch.

Carel stalked around the table, eyeing the precise details the way that a mountain lion studies its prey. It was topographically correct, with every flint upshift and limestone creek bed meticulously sculpted. In place of the existing flats of mesquite brush and gravel pits, however, were tiny replicas of landscaped lawns and scale models of the Hill Country rancheros that would be built there. The first thirty-four rancheros came in five basic styles, all to be sold and built by Geische Land & Development: Real Estate. There was room for horse barns and deer stands and high-fenced pastures where trophy bucks could be farmed, fed, and harvested. That scale model had set Carel back more than it would have cost him to build a couple of those rancheros, but his instincts told him that it was this kind of investment and vision you needed if you were going to play in the world of big-money real estate. Carel was betting his hat on all this.

The model had been used to lure the backing of a syndicate of Houston land developers. Carel had wooed this group of men over several years. They had big-city expertise in real estate development, and they had the resources to get behind such a grand scheme. Carel had the land. And the history.

He had taken these moneyed men deer hunting on the raw land, always making sure they took home a trophy buck that he'd stocked on the sly, fed like a pet, and set out in front of their Leupold VX-6 riflescopes. He put them up in local bed-and-breakfasts and treated them to big, beefy dinners at the town's German restaurants, where he'd tell them Uncle Victor's rodeo stories. The legend of Ranger Creek grew out of these investor briefings—the story of this Geische ranch, back in 1881 or thereabouts, where a company of Texas Rangers from Del Rio made their camp while they waited to ride into the battle that drove the last warring Comanche from the Hill Country and freed all of South Central Texas from the Indian menace—or so the story was told.

"You're not just buying a ranchero in the Texas Hill County," Carel told them. "You're buying a piece of Texas history."

They loved that tagline. They had a big-name Houston ad agency design a marketing campaign around Carel's *You're buying a piece of Texas history* theme. Promotion materials and billboards were waiting to be created. Carel knew he had reached the championship round, but the process had drained him financially. If only he could keep himself afloat long enough to see the deal come together. Now it was all down to a matter of true grit.

Carel downed the last of the tequila and stood before the oval mirror, checking his character and practicing his draw. Six-guns, white hat, and skivvies. Polishing those Ranger skills. It was his heritage. Hadn't he been a good Lutheran son of this town? Giving generously of himself and his money?

Draw!

Click. Click.

And those who came before him—hadn't the Geisches poured their blood and sweat into the soil of Gillespie County for the past hundred years? How did it come to be so difficult to work with his own people? The permits and the surveys and the bickering it took to do something that would be so good for this town. And the obstinate Historical Society. Hell, *he* was the history of this town.

Draw!

Click. Click.

It was all so different now. Back then, all you had to do to leave your mark on Texas history was shoot a bad guy or a bunch of Comanche. Carel stared deeply into the reflected eyes in the mirror, trying to focus on that tequila-blurred image looking back at him: determined and focused, staring down that demon standing between him and his destiny. Just put twenty feet between them, like they did in the old days. The image in the mirror waved in and out of focus. A drunken, hazy image of the bad guy: black shirt, black hat. Deep Spanish eyes. It was none other than Dean Calderon. With palms steady over the pistol grips, Carel didn't let his smile show, but stood firmly planted until the image rippled.

Draw!

Click. Click.

The swiftest draw. The deadliest shot. And the image of Dean Calderon disappeared from the mirror. If only it were that easy.

• • •

In the mirror that hung behind the row of liquor bottles at Buc's Bar and Grill, Mari kept an eye on Dean Calderon as he set aside his pool cue, picked up his beer, and sidled up next to her at the bar—all while she pretended to ignore him. Without looking directly at him, Mari knew that lascivious half-smile was spreading across his face. Even as he leaned into her, she kept her attention on, well, nothing really.

One thing that she liked about him was that he was patient with her. He let her have her moment, before he moved in closer to share a secret.

"Mari." He let the word flow slowly off his tongue with a slight roll on the *r* and a quick departing accent on the *i*. Not a Spanish *Marie* but a name unique to itself. "I know someplace we ain't been yet. Someplace way out there hidden in the night."

She also found it kind of cute the way he'd twist bad song lyrics into pickup lines. She held back her smile, but it must have shown in the glow of her cheeks because Dean was encouraged to press on.

"Someplace we've never been so many, many times before."

He reached out to push a tress of raven-black hair over her ear, out of the way of her silver earring. Still she wouldn't look at him, but nor did she resist. He moved in closer. "It's down some back roads I know. An' there's a moon out there just waitin' for a couple of . . . Well, I'm talkin' about you and me." His arm moved around her shoulder.

Mari spun on her barstool to face him. She had heard those same words come out of the jukebox earlier in the evening. "Dean, I'm not screwin' you in a truck, if that's what you have in mind."

Unfazed, Dean eased back a bit to give her some space, but continued with a line from the chorus: "Am I gonna need you tonight? Where are you when I need you? I . . ." He forgot the rest and just hummed the tune.

When Mari's face broke into something between a smile and a mocking laugh, Dean just said, "Let's blow this joint."

They left Buc's through the Schubert Street stairs, to avoid the Gillespie County sheriff parked in the shadows across from the parking lot, waiting for the DWIs to pull out. Mari and Dean stumbled away, arm in arm and silly-giggling the few blocks to where Dean had left his truck. A southern man, he opened the door for her, borrowing another lyric: "The door's open, but the ride—it ain't free."

Dean's truck was a well-worn Chevy Blazer with dirt on the windshield and dents in the hood. The dashboard was littered with a mess of papers, work gloves, coffee cups, and other things that might have come in handy at one time or another. There were ornaments dangling from the rearview mirror and a "Viva Terlingua" bumper sticker on the roof of the cab. Mari shoved some stuff out of the way and climbed in. Dean rounded to the driver's side, jumped in, and gave her a smile before guiding his truck out through the gravel side streets of the sleeping neighborhood, where there were no cop cars lurking in the shadows.

That's how Dean got to be the trophy buck. He bragged that he could circumnavigate the entire town, "all the way around," without driving on a road that was divided by a white line. He said that as if it were some kind of superpower he possessed.

You don't give directions to a man like that, Mari thought as she rolled down the window to drink in the cool night air. They cruised to the northwest of town on the Old Mason Road and crossed the state highway at the Cherry Mountain Loop, rolling along the unmarked, two-lane blacktop into the darker parts of the Hill Country—all the while pulling a moonlit cloud of caliche dust down the road behind them. Willie Nelson on the radio was nice at first, but the DJ seemed too stuck on him. Dean was lip-synching when Mari reached out and switched the radio off, pronouncing, "A little bit of Willie goes a long way."

Before Dean could cop a mood, she laid her foggy head against his shoulder.

"It's cooled a bit," he said, trying to start a conversation.

"Just drive, baby," she mumbled back.

He slid his right hand onto her thigh, letting his smallest finger slide under the frayed cuff of her denim shorts. She lent no encouragement, no discouragement, and kept her head cocked against his shoulder.

"These roads are all ours in the nighttime," he said, as if that was something deep and poetic.

"Yeah," she mumbled. "Too bad none of them go anywhere, really."

"Oh, they're not meant to take you anywhere, girl. They're just meant to drive on."

"If it ain't some stoplight, it's a fence gate or a bar ditch," Mari murmured. "Even a mountain or an ocean, if you go far enough. Whatever it is that gets in your way just gets bigger and bigger."

Dean took his hand from Mari's leg and moved it around her shoulder. "You just don't worry about getting off to some other place, girl. This here is home to us." He looked down at her to see if she was up for a kiss.

Mari turned her face away and closed her eyes and just said, "Home."

They hit a low water crossing near the old gypsum mine, rattled across a loose cattle guard, and bounced through Metzger Creek, always dry this time of year.

"So why even bother?" Mari asked in a whisper, not really wanting to hear an answer.

But Dean had an answer for everything. "Just do it so we can slip into town every once in a while. Drink a little whisky. Get laid every now and again. Go dancin' at Luckenbach."

He let a mile or so go by, and Mari hoped that he was done talking. But Dean rambled on in a more serious tone.

"Really, babe, take a look at all these new folks movin' into town with all their money an' all. All they want is what you already got. An old house in the Hill Country. You got your daddy's place. See, you are already better off than the whole lot of 'em."

Mari snapped into instant sobriety when a whitetail deer leapt into the cone of their headlights—freezing there, just waiting to be smashed. Dean's steady hand dodged the collision, and they both watched as the young buck hurdled gracefully past their fender and disappeared into the night. Good thing, too, because they both knew Dean had no collision insurance on his truck.

The deer that scared Mari was not the young spike out on the road; rather, it was the one that you couldn't see. She had learned from her daddy that wherever there was a buck in the road, willing to put a dent in your bumper, there would be a doe or two in the mesquite shrub, startled enough to bound into your windshield and total your car.

"One time, out there, my daddy killed a wild boar for me." Mari faced out the window—her words meant for no one.

Dean had heard her. "Right there?"

"No. Not in that exact spot." Mari turned to him. "But out there." She gestured with a toss of her head. "Saved me from getting all gored up, I suppose."

They bumped along without words over the cattle guards at the dilapidated Crabapple schoolhouse, where the road started to wind through some flat pastures of trampled Bermuda grass.

The memory of the boar stayed with Mari. "When I was a little kid, I always wanted to get out into these hills, but my mom and dad wouldn't have it," she told Dean. "These hills had a pull on me like magic. But not after that one time."

He looked over to her like he was due a full explanation.

"Daddy had his rifle," she went on. "That old lever-action Winchester that still sits in my kitchen closet . . . Think that was my *opa*'s gun too. Been in the house forever."

"Ya out huntin' with Mr. Hilss?"

"Not really. Something been killing our sheep. Daddy thought it was some kinda big cat." She paused a bit, recalling that day. "We was trompin' around, and I guess I was the one who scared 'em up. Daddy was behind me. Way behind me." Somehow that memory made her flinch.

Dean stayed quiet, patient.

"When that ugly boar came a-chargin' downhill right at me, with that bristly snout and all them curved teeth and all . . ."

She looked over at Dean, who held her in his eyes, not watching the road. "Dean, I swear to this day, I heard that bullet whizzing right over the top of my head."

"Really?"

"I tell you, it made one bloody mess out of that pig. Daddy got that poor beast just in time. Smacked dead on the ground right there in front of me, so close I could reach out and almost touch it, with all that blood oozing through the dirt right down at me. Scared the piss out of me. And I mean that literally. I was just a little kid then."

The truck hit some gravel on the side of the road, and Dean returned his attention to driving. He said something that Mari didn't hear.

"I was a-cryin' in the dirt 'cause I'd just peed my pants, and my daddy came and squatted next to me, and you know what my daddy said?"

"What?" he answered softly.

Mari closed her eyes for a moment to be sure she got this right. "He pointed up to where that pig had come from, from where we could hear the squealing of some little baby piglets that we just orphaned. And my daddy was wiping on my eyes with that sweaty old bandanna of his, and he says to me: 'That ol' pig just doin' the same thing as me. Just a mama tryin' to look out for her kids.'"

Mari took a deep breath and looked out into the night, where the moonlight silhouetted the slow roll of the hills. "This is a hard land we live on, Mr. Calderon." Dean pulled her in closer to his side, and she was surprised to find tears welling up in her eyes. "Why does everything have to be so damn hard?"

"What's so hard about it?"

She turned her face toward his. "Well, puttin' up with you men, for one thing."

• • •

When Dean dropped off Mari at her house, she gave him a quick good-night kiss in the cab of his truck and sent him on his way. Inside, she found Willow sprawled awkwardly across the sofa, swallowed up by a loose-fitting pullover, occasionally snoring. The TV was on but its sound was off, and the radio provided a juxtaposed soundtrack to the flickering images on the screen. A faint scent of marijuana hung in the air.

Mari found a place to sit on the sofa and moved some tangles of hair from Willow's face without waking her. Mari could never imagine them not living together, but then again, she never thought of anything beyond next month's bills. There were eighteen years between them, but as Willow grew older it seemed that they had become closer in age—like they were two grown-ups living together.

Mari reached out to gently slide the long sleeves up Willow's arms, just to have a look at the old cuts, to participate in her daughter's pain. Nothing made Mari feel more like an inadequate mother than these dainty little scars—just fractions of an inch above that delicate blue artery at Willow's elbow.

Her touch startled Willow awake.

"Get away! Leave me alone. Damn it." Willow recoiled angrily, slapping frantically at her mother's hands.

Mari backed away. "Sweetheart. I was only trying—"

"Don't touch me!" Willow snapped, and she pulled herself into the corner of the couch, folding her arms tightly across herself. "You're drunk. Leave me alone."

Mari took a breath, slowly stood up, and retreated into the kitchen. That anger, too, was what it was like between the two of them.

There was cold water in the fridge but no ice in the freezer.

That girl never refilled the ice trays. After pouring a glass of water Mari spun around, intending to go back and lay a scolding on her insolent daughter, but instead she found Willow stumbling into the kitchen, wiping the sleep from her eyes.

"Got the B and B all cleaned up," Willow told her. "Ready for those guys. They said they would be in early tomorrow, didn't they? Or is that today already? Hell, if they're going to be that early, they could show up anytime now, couldn't they? Where did you say they were from?"

"Um . . . Up north. Denton or someplace 'round there. I think." The mood had changed from fight-ready to affable mother-daughter sweetness. "Here, do you want some water? It's cold."

Willow took the water and sat at the table. Mari fetched another glass for herself before she took a chair.

"It's too hot to bake anything for them," Mari offered. "If they're driving all the way down from Denton, I'll just pick up something at Dietz's Bakery in the morning. They won't care."

"Won't care? Bunch of Yankees. They won't know."

Mari looked out through the kitchen window, recalling what Dean had said on the ride home, about her daddy's ranch. The first permanent structure erected on the Hilss farmstead had been a Sunday house, a highly efficient limestone structure that so many German settlers in this area put up, with two stories in front and a long, sloping roof that dropped to one story in the back. The taller roof in front allowed for a loft where the children would sleep when the ranch families made their way into town for market day on Saturday and stayed for church on Sunday. Like all the Sunday houses in Gillespie County, this one was constructed of limestone blocks—cool in the summer, warm in the winter—and built so solid, it wasn't ever going to come down.

This was the sturdy little building that the earlier Hilsses had lived in when first working this land. Mari's father had used it for storage mostly. When Willow was little, Mari had cleaned out the Sunday house, filled it with old furniture and knickknacks from around the farm, and rented it out as a bed-and-breakfast for visitors who came for the fairs and festivals that made this old German community so attractive. It turned out to be something of a living for the little family, and it was a lot easier than farming. Mari leased out the pastures to an old friend of her father who still ran some sheep out there. That kept the fields from becoming overgrown and added a rural feel to the bed-and-breakfast experience, but it didn't bring in much money.

The two of them also kept up with the family's little orchard of freestone peach trees that Ted Hilss and his dad had put in when Mari was just a toddler. The orchard was a lot of work that brought them a little pocket money in the summer, and they put up some of the sweet canned peaches, which Willow was now plucking from a jar, letting the sticky syrup ooze down her fingers.

"Is Dean here?" Willow asked just before she sucked the juice from a peach slice.

"No, he just dropped me."

"Then where's the truck?"

"I left it at Buc's."

"That's my truck, Mama. Dad gave it to me."

"Yes, honey. But I'm the only one that's been putting gas in it. And who's making the insurance payments?"

Willow gave her mother a fake parental scowl. "So when you getting your Jeep fixed?"

"I am always getting that damn Jeep fixed." Mari got up and kissed her daughter on the forehead. "I'm going to bed."

"Where are the keys?" Willow shouted after her.

"Under the seat."

"Great."

"Don't go worrying about that," Mari called from down the hall. "There are more cops watching Buc's than there are watching the president of the United States."

The only room in their house that had decent air-conditioning was the master bedroom. Mari was already in bed when Willow cracked the door. "Hey, Mom. Can I sleep in here tonight?"

"Sure thing, sweetie. I always have a place for you."

Willow lay down on the bed next to her mother. "Yeah. If Dean was here, would you throw him out for me?" she teased.

Mari tossed back the bedsheet to make room. "I already done that."

A Night in
Old Fredericksburg

First time out as a couple, and it occurred to Thea that they were well beyond the age when it might be called "dating." She had come back to Fredericksburg to start a business after a full decade in Austin, with furrowed brow and a demonic focus on the success of her venture—like she had something to prove. She was caught off guard when, after a tedious meeting about advertising credits for her upscale lingerie store in the Historic District of this rock-rimmed old Lutheran town, Brady Casbier had asked her out. A gawky dolt of a guy she had avoided in high school, he gave her a business card that read:

Temporary Assistant Managing Editor
Fredericksburg Standard Radio-Post

After granting her every discount and concession she requested, he had just leaned across his desk and asked her to join him for a glass of wine that evening. She'd surprised herself by accepting.

She cast a glance now over the patio at the wine bar on the corner of San Antonio and Lincoln streets, anxious to find out who might be snooping on them. Approaching the entrance, they must have come off as an odd pair: him gangly and towering, and her pulling at her evening dress to mitigate her plumpness. One thing she missed about her former city life was the anonymity of the dating scene. Although she had come home on a different mission, she felt that she might be ready to put herself out there again and considered this a trial run. Besides, it was well past the era when a lady needed to be "involved with" someone in order to share a glass a wine with him, or even to take him to bed. *We're grownups*, she assured herself. This could even be a business dinner.

Standing beside her, Brady seemed quite pleased with himself, dressed up in a fresh-out-of-the-box shirt that still had the factory creases, and rambling on with his winsome tale of his almost-teenage daughter at home with pizza and some rented videos to keep peace with her younger brother.

"Telephone number's clipped to the refrigerator." He seemed to revel in the trivial rites of fatherhood. "Just in case."

Unfamiliar with the rituals of parenting, Thea nodded and smiled politely.

"Not that anything would happen," he said.

"What could happen? This is Fredericksburg." She shrugged, still with a pushed smile.

"Gives her a sense of security. And confidence."

"Of course."

"Now Miguel, he has no sense of fear at all."

He wasn't going to stop talking about his kids, she realized. Everyone seemed to admire Brady's status as a single, never-been-married father of two adopted kids, as though it spoke to some core virtue within him. Thea found it just plain weird.

They hadn't even seen a waiter, and already she felt stuck.

They took a seat at one of the wrought-iron tables along the sidewalk but still under the arbors, and sent a waiter for some wine and a plate of fruit and cheese.

Desperate to change the conversation, Thea jumped to the one thing they had in common. "Did I get you in trouble with the ad credit?"

"No. I got it approved. It's all okay." He cocked his head and smiled in a peculiar way. "Or I wouldn't have asked you out."

She wasn't sure how to take that response. "I know you worked hard on it," she said. "I just need to get it right next week. With all the visitors in town for the county fair, it's an important time for sales."

"Don't I know it. We hear that from everyone." Brady's pat response was not reassuring. "So, *damen unterwasche.* We will never get the spelling right." He leaned in toward her with exaggerated seriousness. "It just doesn't want to be there."

Thea took offense at his remark, but she chose to ride on the playful side of the conversation. The sign on her door was designed to evoke a certain curiosity:

intimates
DAMEN UNTERWASCHE

"Carel suggested it," Thea responded in a neutral tone. "He was so helpful in getting me into that location. He was so involved. Almost took over the whole project. It was like I owed him something for his efforts."

"Carel Geische? Very persuasive, but not always right, you know."

"He said adding the *damen unterwasche* under the name made the shop look so much more German."

Brady laughed. "But Carel overlooked the fact that the old German *damen* of Fredericksburg buy their *unterwasche* in packs of six down at the Walmart."

"But"—Thea raised a finger to emphasize her master stroke—"the tourists don't know that."

The cocky expression fell from Brady's face, and he nodded slowly. "And the tourists are your market. I see the wisdom in that." His eyes lingered on hers.

He was sincere. Thea appreciated Brady's yielding response and suddenly felt a lot less stuck. "Also, I needed to tone down the sexy side and focus on the fine lingerie aspect instead."

"Oh, Thea. There is nothing that kills 'sexy' like *damen unterwasche*."

They shared a laugh as the evening drew itself up along the sun-bleached limestone walls across the narrow street and those ancient buildings took on a softer, yellow hue. Sparkling, burgundy-style glasses were set on the table before them, and an enticing stream of pale, almost copper-pink wine flowed over the rims and pooled in the broad bowls—rich and distinctively floral.

"There are many Texas varietals that I will not pour, but this . . ." Wearing his white apron, crisp as a nun's habit, over shorts and a T-shirt, Ross—the faux sommelier and primary personality of this wine bar—leaned forward to decant with a rehearsed finesse. "This is a first-class pinot grigio, vinted not far from here."

The wine bar on Lincoln Street was not a place where familiar customers chose their own wine. Ross served what he selected for his friends. His eyes shifted off for a moment, like a play actor's, pretending to let them know he was about to share a deep secret. "An early grape for this part of Texas, difficult to finish correctly, but if a vintner can get past that early sweetness and ferment to dryness you get"—with a flair—"this." He broke off the pour with a quick twist of his wrist and stood erect as if the enigmatic ceremony was over. "And a decidedly robust alcohol content as well."

Thea kept an eye on Brady as he picked up his glass, holding it up to the light and sniffing at it, assuming the guise of an aficionado. Thea reached slowly for hers, taking it by the stem and pausing with the glass just before her lips.

"You can't appreciate the body of grigio without a good nose." Ross was holding a glass that he had poured for himself, raising it out before him like a toastmaster might, and swirling the wine around the inside of the bowl. "You have to get your nose deeply into it. Don't be shy." Following his example, each of them sniffed at their glasses like curious beagles. Ross sipped deeply. "Crisp. Refreshing. Like the Oregon pinots. But still rich, don't you think?"

"Ross?" Brady interrupted his performance. "Am I paying for that wine you're drinking?"

Ross held to his script. "Yes. I like it—somewhat floral, and notice that it weeps just a bit. The body is in the nose."

The body is in the nose? Thea nearly spewed out her wine in a burst of laughter at the mental image. Her cheeks flushed red and her eyes teared up as she struggled, embarrassed, to hold her rude laughter in. She quickly put a napkin to her face, relieved to see that Brady, too, was trying to hold back his laugh.

Ross continued to study his glass for a moment, then launched into the next monologue in his repertoire. "And you, my friend—our journalistic champion." His hand was on

Brady's shoulder. "You, who put it so well in that extraordinary piece of muckraking you wrote. How refreshing that your paper, the bastion of reactionary Fredericksburg, would dig its head out of the sand and have the balls to tell people what is really going on around here." Balancing the wine bottle and the burgundy glass in his hand, Ross reeled in a pirouette to bring his face so close to Thea that it startled her. "Did you read this man's article? 'Tuscany in Texas'?"

Thea nodded rapidly, though she hadn't read it.

"I quoted Ross in the article." Brady directed his words toward her, explaining Ross's exuberance. "Twice."

"And I'm nominating you for a Pulitzer, my friend." Ross bowed and took his show to another table.

"So your article was well received. What exactly was it about?" When Brady's face twisted up like a wrung washcloth, Thea admitted she'd just wanted to get Ross out of her face.

Brady nodded, took a drink, and leaned back in his chair before starting in. "Well, it's not so much about the success of the small vineyards scattered throughout the county. Rather, it's more of—"

Thea leaned in and laid a light touch of her hand on his forearm. "Hey, look. Here they are." She tilted her head toward two new arrivals sashaying across the flagstone and yapping like cousins, which they were. "I mentioned that I might be here this evening." Actually, Thea had invited Jeanie and Gerdie in the event that her date with Brady went awry.

The cousins ducked into the shade of the arbor, a couple of single-again mothers matching each other in their denim shorts, tank tops, and layered jewelry ringing their necks and wrists, each of them lugging a jumbo-sized cloth purse. Imogene Geische and Gertrude Ritzi were their given names, before expunging the obtuse German branding that they had inherited. Although she'd been born one of those Fredericksburg kids herself, Thea was given a short, inflexible name and thus was spared the work of modernizing it. In her uncomfortably tight skirt, she felt a bit overdressed and under-jeweled.

Mischievous and attractive, Jeanie walked right up to Brady and swatted him with a folded newspaper like she would punish a dog. "So what's with this 'Tuscany in Texas' stuff, Brady Casbier? I thought you grew up here, like the rest of us. Now what are you saying here? We're French?"

"Italy," Brady responded as Jeanie settled herself into the chair between him and Thea.

Gerdie crossed behind Thea to get to the empty chair on the far side. As she squeezed past, she leaned into Thea to touch cheeks with a whispered greeting and a smile.

"Tuscany is in Italy, not France." Brady turned toward Thea and shrugged. "This is what most of the feedback has been."

From behind her burgundy glass, Thea threw him a smile that was meant to convey: *You are on your own here, mister.*

Gerdie heaved her large purse on the table and chimed in. "So now, Tuscany is here in Texas. Is that what you're saying?"

"Yes," Brady conceded, "that's it."

"You mean they're moving here?" Jeanie asked. "From Italy?"

"No!" Brady was using his hands to explain. "It's about wine. The story is about wine!" He looked from one of the cousins to the other. "Did you actually read the article?"

Both Gerdie and Jeanie shook their heads in unison, and the entire table fell into the doldrums.

Jeanie seemed to feel the need to apologize. "Didn't mean to be so nitpicky, Brady."

"You weren't being nitpicky, Jeanie," Gerdie said soothingly.

"This, on the other hand, is exceptionally nitpicky." Ross had magically reappeared with two new glasses. He took a position between Gerdie and Thea, pausing until he had the table's undivided attention. "This is a newly released pinot grigio from a small vineyard I discovered out in Menard County. Cool and crisp. Perfect for a warm Texas evening."

Gerdie lifted the corner of his apron, peeking to see what lay underneath. "I like your skirt, Ross. Cool and crisp. Perfect for a warm Texas evening."

The table erupted in laughter, Ross included, and a cork came out of another bottle. Thea knew that the last laugh was his. That grigio he was pushing was quite expensive and going on Brady's tab.

Wine was the day's release for all of them—not just at Thea and Brady's table, but for all the local couples and the bevy of tourists who drifted up under the arbor, looking for a shady place to sit. The volume of the background chatter rose steadily until Thea could no longer hear the melodies of the local bluesman, who was perched with his Les Paul guitar on a kitchen stool at the far side of the patio. The white noise insulated Thea from the prattle at her own table, cheap gossip that jumped from topic to topic—the strange antics of other people's children, who had been messing around with whom—like pressing the buttons on an old car radio.

The table where they sat was close enough to the street that, on occasion, their gab would be drowned out by the bone-rattling clamor of a diesel truck growling down Lincoln Street. One in particular shouldered its way, back and forth, into a parking spot that was suitable for a compact car. Headlights cut, truck doors slammed, and two new figures stepped into the patio light: Mari Hilss and Dean Calderon.

With a grin the size of the moon crossing his face, Brady rose from his seat and signaled to his old schoolmates with a flick of his wrist. Jeanie buried her head in the crook of her elbow and melted into her chair, muttering, "What on earth did I do to deserve this?"

With no predispositions of her own, Thea drew down a deep mouthful of pinot grigio to brace herself for another clash of small-town histories.

Dean and Mari, bubbly and stumbling, wormed their way across the crowded patio. Gerdie rose with a cheerful embrace for Mari, while Jeanie crossed her arms and turned away, positioning herself to obstruct Brady from greeting his old pals. Brady worked his gangly frame past Jeanie and took Mari in his arms—a demonstrative hug they held for too long. Thea, seated on the far side of the table, got by with a wave and a smile.

Dean cut a striking figure in his night-on-the-town T-shirt, which did a good job of showing off his muscular, working-man biceps but finished with the disappointment of a pot-belly that hung out enough to hide his belt buckle. He called across the table to his ex-wife. "You didn't tell me you were getting in this early."

While the other girls were eyeing his physique, Jeanie pretended to ignore him.

He pressed on. "You got Caitlin with you?"

"I wouldn't bring Caitlin to a bar, Dean. She's with family."

"I could have taken her if you'd let me know you were getting in so early. I wasn't expecting you 'til this weekend."

"She's better off where she's at."

"Better off with your brother?" Fingers of jet-black hair crossed his brow as he cocked his head. "You seen how good he did at raising his own daughter. What do you think he's gonna be doin' with Caitlin?"

Gerdie chimed in to diffuse the tension. "Carel was going to show her how to make margaritas. A skill that will serve you both well into your senior years." If anyone found that funny, they didn't laugh.

Mari took Dean's elbow. "Let's you and me go inside for a spell. They got the air-conditioning on," she said, leading him away. Over her shoulder, she left them with a smile and a wave of fluttering fingertips.

Gerdie turned to goad her cousin, who was puckered up and fuming. "That's why I had my kids in San Antonio. You don't run into this." She fluttered her own fingers in the air, mocking Mari's departing wave. "My ex stays down there."

Jeanie kept her squint-eyed glower on Brady, who was trying to get back to his chair without banging into her. With a slur to her words, she blurted out, "There is no way in hell that I am going to let my daughter end up like her."

"Like who?" asked Brady as he took his seat. "Mari?"

Jeanie answered with a tsk-tsk in her voice. "No. Who cares about that bitch?" She jerked her thumb over her shoulder toward the inside bar. Everyone's eyes tracked her gesture.

"Which bitch do you mean, then?" Even Gerdie wasn't following her cousin.

"Her daughter, of course. I'm talking about Carel's daughter. Willow. The one with the thing in her nose. Carel would have never stood for that."

"Well, he did, didn't he?" Brady's words stopped the conversation and earned the ire of both cousins.

Jeanie bore into him with her intense frown.

"Carel is the girl's father." Brady met Jeanie's eyes. "He lives here. They're in the same damn town. It wasn't Willow who walked out on him."

"Why, you son of a bitch," Jeanie snapped. "Carel did

whatever he could to raise that little tramp. But she had to go side with her mom, and now she's all screwed up, and it is just killing Carel to see his own daughter like that. I know. He talks to me about all that stuff."

Brady said nothing more, while Jeanie and Gerdie launched into a private quarrel about Carel and Mari's divorce and how Willow had turned out.

Thea leaned into her wine. She wasn't going to get involved in this. She did think back to her one encounter with the Geische girl. And, yes, she found her to be unsophisticated, a small-town girl—not unlike the rest of them at that age.

Coming into intimates, the young girl had said she was looking for some "sexy undies that would turn *him* on." She'd held up a pair of scant T-back panties and examined the garment as if it was a pelt, not at all delicate. "So this is all there is to cover your junk?"

"Junk?" That may have been the edge the cousins were going on about—a revealing little piece of trash talk. But there was something in Willow's manner that reminded Thea of her sessions with a therapist in Austin. That therapist had tried to convince Thea that she had been abused as a child—not overtly, like she was beaten or molested, but rather that she had been ignored in a large family of modest means. Thea had never reconciled herself to the idea, but when Willow came into her shop, something triggered that random recollection of her long-forgotten therapist.

Thea had redirected her customer's attention with a learned sales response. "You want to buy lingerie for *you*. So that you feel good about yourself. You don't buy lingerie for *him*."

A baffled and innocent look overtook Willow's face at that moment, and her curious eyes bore into Thea. Something in that expression gave Thea, for an instant, the impression that there was more to Willow than met the eye—that there was something deep and contemplative inside this naïve girl.

Then Thea had added, without a hint of humor in her voice, "Unless, of course, he's a cross-dresser."

Willow's explosive laugh had alarmed her. She'd recoiled when the girl had leapt forward to wrap her in a bear hug, right there in the store. More than a clasp of kinship, it was an embrace of enduring affinity that was almost sexual, like the secret handshake of a cult. It had lasted a little too long—very much like the one Thea had just witnessed between Brady and Mari.

The cousins' quarrel eventually reached a stalemate, and they became best friends once again. The ladies, with their glasses empty, looked around for Ross, who was entertaining another table. When Brady excused himself to go questing for more wine, the ladies raked their eyes over the back of his new shirt as he disappeared into the jungle of wine enthusiasts. He was fair game now.

Jeanie dove in first. "Did you see how he stumbled all over me just to cop a feel from his old girlfriend?"

Casting for yet another piece of the puzzle, Thea asked, innocently enough, "I don't remember Brady dating Mari back in high school."

"Some big debt of gratitude, I'm sure," Jeanie scoffed. "I'll bet you she was his first, if you know what I mean."

"No," Gerdie shot back. "It was Gus. Brady's big brother, remember? Gus Casbier. Football guy? Gus went out with Mari. High school sweethearts, gonna get married and all. Then he went off in the army and got killed someplace. Remember? We had that big memorial. The high school band played at his funeral."

"So, they're kind of wrapped up together in one of those platonic death-slash-affection kind of things." Jeanie rolled her eyes with dramatic exaggeration. "Whatever it is, he just has to get over it. He's as touched as she is."

Gerdie nudged Jeanie under the table, and both of them suddenly cast a contrite glance toward Thea.

Thea picked up on it quickly. "Oh, no. It's not like that at all. We're not involved or anything. I just buy advertising from him," she said and it was the truth. But she had to admit, to herself, that she had been somewhat impressed: Brady was strong enough to take a stand among friends and then hold his tongue when that was the right thing to do.

The table fell quiet as Brady made his way back. "Check this out," he grinned. "It's their last bottle, but I got it." Standing between Thea and Gerdie, he took on the airs of the sommelier and attempted to pour with the same flourish, except he managed to miss two of the glasses and slopped some on Jeanie's hands.

"Okay, then." Brady filled his glass last and lifted it up to the light to study it. He sniffed at its bouquet and took a drink, and with a deeply satisfied expression, he held his glass out to them as a toast. "The body"—he looked deep into Thea's eyes—"remains in the nose."

Thea laughed out loud while the two cousins exchanged perplexed looks. When Brady steadied himself on the arm of her chair, Thea had to stifle a momentary pang of affection, or maybe respect. She saw something purposeful in him, something that contradicted his big, ungainly mannerisms. Maybe the wine had tripped her hormones. At the same time, she was hoping he wouldn't try to sit in her lap. She reached out to give his hand a little squeeze and noticed that it took him by surprise.

"Thanks for this"—she paused to carefully choose her word—"beautiful wine."

Brady was glazed over. "It's a kick-ass wine."

The two cousins raised their glasses and toasted in unison. "It's a kick-ass wine."

Thea's pleasant euphoria was stolen away when she went inside in search of the ladies' room and was immediately swallowed up by the crowd. Being pressed against people in embarrassing ways made her especially self-conscious of her larger size as she maneuvered her way into the line. Mari was directly across from her, not in line but perched at the end of the wine counter.

"We'll be seeing you out at Luckenbach tonight?" Mari shouted.

Thea managed a cordial smile at the unwanted attention. What she wanted most was to be anywhere else.

Mari pressed her inebriated kinship and elbowed her way to join Thea, who now regretted her affable wave earlier that evening.

"This is our dinner," Mari hollered out, even though her face was just a few inches from Thea's. "And after this we're going to do some drinking."

Some of the other folks standing about found that humorous and added a boisterous barroom laugh, letting Thea know that everyone was aware she was standing in the bathroom line.

Mari slid up closer to Thea and stage-whispered, "Brady's a good guy. I hope you've found something that you can really like about him."

"Why, that's nice of you to say, Mari. I think." Thea tried to move away from Mari's alcohol breath.

Mari held her arm, her bloodshot stare boring into Thea. "He's the kind of guy that would kill a pig for you."

Thea pushed ahead rather forcefully and finally made it into the privacy of the tiny commode stall, where she could catch her breath. Kill a pig for you? What was that, some kind of redneck idiom? Mari had said it as if it were a good thing.

Finally alone, with her panties at her ankles and her hand on the walls to keep them from spinning, Thea wondered what had happened to her hometown since she had been away. While the town itself had become so much more attractive and sophisticated, the people here—her childhood friends— all seemed so downright strange to her. Adults, with children of their own, who were still stuck in high school. Thea just wanted to scream.

• • •

"Caitlin's all fussy. Says she wants a chicken-fried steak," Cora Lynn told Carel on the phone. "Seems her mama told her that when they got to Fredericksburg, her Uncle Carel would buy her a chicken-fried steak. Can you imagine?"

Carel was out in the county, doing something at Ranger Creek—not that there was anything to be done out there—and Cora Lynn had to leave work to take care of her sister-in-law's kid because dear Jeanie had made plans to meet up with some of her cousins.

"She's six years old," Cora Lynn was saying. "She can't eat a chicken-fried steak."

Carel could tell that his wife had already copped a sour mood for the evening. "Hell, Cora Lynn. At six years old, she doesn't even know what a chicken-fried steak is. Let's take her out and show her one. Why don't you bundle her into your car, and I'll meet you down at Oma Kooks in a half hour. They've got that clear Mexican *añejo* . . . and Uncle Carel would like to buy *you* one of those margaritas."

Over the phone he could hear her smile, or so he thought.

"Half an hour? I'm not going to wait for you to order. You just be sure to get there before the check comes."

Oma Kooks was a long, open hall of a restaurant with a well-stocked bar near the clunky doors that opened onto Main Street. An old vaudeville-type stage at the far end featured a solo guitarist or a package show from time to time. With walls of limestone block and high ceilings, it was loud even without a band.

When Carel came through the door about an hour later, Caitlin was sitting behind a large plate of chicken-fried steak, and Cora Lynn had two salt-rimmed margarita glasses on the table in front of her. One was almost empty.

"So how you like it, Caitlin?" he asked.

"It's big." The squirrely girl grinned, pushing a french fry through the white gravy—the only part of her meal that she had touched.

Carel kissed them both—Caitlin on the forehead, Cora Lynn on the cheek—before taking his seat and reaching for the untouched margarita.

"That's my second one." Cora Lynn slapped his hand away. "You can order your own."

Carel signaled the waitress. "I'll have two of those. I see I have some catching up to do." He watched her ass-tight jeans as she walked away, his thoughts flashing to his own daughter and how men his age kept their eyes on her after she took their order.

Cora Lynn brought his attention back to the table. "I was talking to the boys about when we might want to go out to the fair together. Make it a family day and all. Can you find out what your sister is planning to do? We can all go together, or meet out there. Either way. But I don't want to be out there all willy-nilly—always looking for each other."

"Sure. Just tell me when, and I'll tell Jeanie to be there."

"I'm not trying to be the trail boss here," Cora Lynn snipped. "I just want it to be a nice family day."

Two new margaritas arrived, and Carel took a long, hard drink from the first one, forcing himself to keep his eyes off the waitress.

"Wow, Uncle Carel. You drink fast," Caitlin said while pushing french fries through her white gravy. Still not a bite from her chicken-fried steak. "Can I taste some?"

"Not until you finish your dinner."

"It's too big," Caitlin pouted.

"Here, sweetheart. You have your own drink." Cora Lynn passed her sippy cup to her, then looked at Carel. "Maybe you should have ordered yours in a sippy cup."

Carel teased her with a smile. "They're not big enough."

After getting Caitlin straightened out, Cora Lynn returned to the plans for the fair. "Anyhoo, Jordan wants to bring that Keubel girl he's been seeing along with us. That's a big thing, you know. It's kind of like a next step in a relationship that's getting serious."

"Really?"

"Yes. It's like he's fixin' to introduce her to the family."

"We know the Keubels already. All of 'em."

"This is kind of a formal step. It's important to Jordan, and he wanted to be sure it was okay with you."

Carel started in on his second margarita. "Well, sure. It's fine with me. I look forward to getting to know her better."

"Thank you, sugar." She stroked his thigh under the table.

"This also gives me a reason to make a phone call I've been trying to get around to."

"What's that?"

"I'll call Willow. Ask her along."

Cora Lynn retracted her hand. "Willow? Why her?"

"Like you said, it's a family thing. She's my daughter."

Cora Lynn's face twisted wicked. "She never came before. I don't see how she'd want anything to do with us. I don't see how you can even count her in our family."

"She's my blood, Cora Lynn." Carel's voice boomed throughout the restaurant. "If you want to go questioning who's family or not, we should start with Jordan and Justin. There is not a drop of Geische blood running through them. Just Geische money."

People at other tables paused to watch, and Carel could see Caitlin stiffen amid the growing tension. With a glance at his wife, he sat back in his chair and took a breath. Those dining around them returned to their own conversations.

"Voices sure carry in here," Carel said, trying to tone it down. "You want another drink?"

"I'm fine," she said, but he knew that she wasn't. "We can talk about this later."

They sat there, trying to cajole Caitlin into tasting her chicken-fried steak. Carel ordered another margarita with a straight shot of clear Mexican *añejo* on the side. After downing the shot, he made an effort to take their conversation back to neutral ground. "Why did things seem so much more clear in the old days? The way this town was when all the families still spoke German."

"My family didn't speak German," Cora Lynn added.

"If this was just one generation back," he went on, "you and I wouldn't be sitting around a table trying to figure out who was family and who wasn't. We'd know, and so would everyone else."

"Maybe so, Carel. Maybe so."

When Cora Lynn started to gather up Caitlin, getting

ready to leave, Carel added one more wrinkle to their predicament. "I want to add Willow in the ownership trust for Ranger Creek."

Cora Lynn's jaw dropped.

"Your sons are included," he continued. "I want to include my daughter."

Cora Lynn scooped Caitlin out of her chair and gathered up her purse. "We'll talk about this later, Carel. You get the check."

Before they were out of the door, Carel called the waitress and ordered another margarita. As she walked away, he called after her, "No, change that. Just bring me two shots."

· · ·

What is history but a mark set in the ground by a man furtive enough to set it there? Carel Geische saw himself as such a man. He was hard at work, way past midnight, out on the Hilmar Jung Road—a poorly maintained caliche road that cut its way along Palo Alto Creek, connecting two properly paved county roads. It was an inconspicuous place for a Texas state historical marker. No one came by here, but there was a run-down old farmhouse where some big-name Dallas lawyer had come along and turned it into a bed-and-breakfast for a few years, petitioned the Texas Historical Commission for a historical marker, and gotten it. When the *auslanders* lost interest, they'd abandoned the bed-and-breakfast and moved on, but the historical marker stayed there. That just wasn't right.

Carel had a night's worth of clear Mexican *añejo* in him, and the sparks were flying after those cross words with that unappreciative woman he had married. Now he was using an acetylene torch to cut through the metal pole that held this isolated historical marker. He would have looked odd to anyone who might have passed by, still in the starched white shirt and his ostrich-skin Lucchese boots, but with a welder's helmet covering his head. Unable to keep the oxygen mixture right, and struggling to make a straight cut, he was finding out exactly how difficult it was to take history into his own hands.

An official Texas state historical marker would have been a great boon for Ranger Creek, a tangible foundation of his marketing tagline: *You're Buying a Piece of Texas History*. The University of Texas at Austin seated an eminent Texas historian who had a reputation for his revisionist interpretations of Texas history. It was that "revision" of Texas history that led Carel to pay the esteemed professor a summer's retainer to research and provide a more favorable interpretation of a minor piece of Texas history in Gillespie County.

What Carel learned for his money was that his great-great-grandfather had never been in the Texas Rangers; that the German pioneers of Gillespie County enjoyed an unbroken history of peaceful relationships with the Comanche; and that the battle in 1881, which Uncle Victor had colored and personalized for him as a youth, was nothing more than a running shoot-'em-up between a few ranchers and a small group of transient Indians. And that it had taken place up in Llano County, nearly sixty miles away.

"Couldn't you just move it down a little further south?" Carel had asked the professor. "I mean, couldn't some of them have ridden down into Gillespie County?"

Carel found the arrogant pinhead to be a disappointing waste of his time, and he watched more of his money vanish into history as he realized that there had never been a Texas Ranger at Ranger Creek.

"*Gott verdammte Sie!*" A raucous blast of profanity echoed through the night as Carel threw the torch to the ground. The welder's helmet flew into the roadway, and Carel kicked at the metal pole again and again. It didn't budge. He slouched to the ground, brushing at himself where an errant spark had burnt through his shirt and scorched his skin. It stung badly. *Not defeated*, he told himself, *just reloading*.

"Turn off the torch and set it on the ground, Mr. Geische."

So distracted by his crime, Carel hadn't noticed the Gillespie County sheriff's cruiser pull up behind him. Carel turned his head slowly and took note of Deputy Bobby Ortega's serious posture and the hand that lay on his service revolver. No one ever said making history was easy.

"You don't have a permit for this, do you, Mr. Geische?" Deputy Ortega asked, in a more timid tone this time.

Carel shook his head. "Nope. I didn't know you needed a permit for this."

Ortega placed him under arrest, handcuffed him, and escorted him to the backseat of the cruiser, all the while apologizing. "I'm sorry about the precautions, Mr. Geische, but there is a potential weapon involved." He nodded toward the acetylene torch.

"It's okay, Bobby. I understand."

A second Gillespie County sheriff's car, called in as backup, rolled to the side of the road—no lights, no siren. The second officer was Deputy Lester Metzger, who had gone to school with Carel. The two cops spoke with each other for a moment, and Lester made a call on his cell phone. When Lester approached, Carel greeted him. "How you doing, Lester? Your kids get back from band camp yet?"

"They've been home for a couple weeks now." Lester opened the door to let Carel out. "You're not under arrest, Mr. Geische, but your uncle would like to see you."

Uncuffed, Carel started to amble off toward his truck, parked on the opposite side of the road. "Okay. I'll give him a call."

Lester reached out and took a firm grip on Carel's arm. "I'll give you a ride, Mr. Geische." He wore an official smile. "Your uncle wants to see you right now."

One thing that no one in Fredericksburg wanted to see was Gillespie County Sheriff Otto Geische roused from his bed at two o'clock in the morning. Lester drove Carel to the sheriff's house and waited on the porch as the sheriff opened the screen door and took his nephew inside.

Otto Geische was the older brother of Carel's father and Uncle Victor, and much larger than both of them. One thing Carel hadn't known about his uncle was that he slept in a loose white T-shirt and boxer shorts. Otto had pulled a shirt on but had not buttoned it. His thin, white hair was mussed up, his face still puffy with sleep, and his breath smelled awful from across the room. Even in his pajamas, he conveyed the attitude that he would break you in two if you gave him a reason.

"Here. Take a seat."

Carel sat.

Otto stood over him. "Maybe I'm *Simplifizieren,* Carel, but for the life of me I cannot figure out what the hell has gotten into you." Carel started to answer, but Otto hadn't gotten out of bed at two in the morning to listen to his nephew's excuses. He put his face down near Carel's. "I don't give a crap what is behind these bizarre actions of yours, son. They just have to stop."

"That signpost out there tonight . . . Well, I have no excuses for—"

"*Verdammen du*, that's right you don't!" Otto shouted in Carel's face. "And I don't give a damn about the sign. That's state police business. But what's this about you manhandling the little fella from the Historical Society?"

"Who? Walter? Sure, we had words. I don't know what you heard. I didn't hit him or anything."

"No. You snatched him up like this." In one rough move, Otto gathered Carel up by his shirt collar and lifted him so that his butt was off the seat. The sheriff held him there, effortlessly, for a long, frightening moment, frozen face-to-face, subjecting Carel to his cruel and unusual halitosis. "Something like this, wasn't it?"

"Yes, sir."

Otto dropped Carel back into the chair. "That's assault, son. And tonight, it's willful destruction of state property." Otto had a finger in Carel's face. "If you're trying for a spell down in Huntsville prison, *Gott im Himmel*, I will send you down there. Blood or not."

"No, sir," Carel said, answering an unasked question.

"You got too much going on in this town to screw it up now. If it's your drinking, you get yourself some help. Don't try to explain your problems to me. Just get it fixed. I'm not a social worker, Carel. I'm a cop. And nephew or not, I will mess up the rest of your life."

When Otto took a seat for himself, Carel exhaled for the first time. His uncle had always been the bully of the family and a real Texas lawman.

"You have, in the past, made great contributions to our community and its great heritage, Carel. You put up some nice buildings that we're all proud of. Now I strongly urge you to contact the Texas Historical Commission on your own volition, and offer to restore—at your own expense—the damage that some vandal did to that historical marker." His voice rose at the end. "*Verstehen Sie?*"

"Yes, sir. I will."

With the business at hand completed, Otto relaxed and offered up an avuncular smile. "I hear your sister is on her way up for the fair," he said. "Sure hope she finds the time to stop by for a visit. I'd like to see how that cute little girl of hers is growing up. You make sure you tell Imogene that for me."

"Yes, sir."

"Lester will take you home. You're too alcohol-impaired to be sitting behind the wheel of an automobile." He turned to his bedroom. "You can fetch your truck tomorrow, Carel. It'll be safe out there tonight. Nobody crosses over Hilmar Jung Road at night unless they're up to no good."

• • •

Although Willow and her boyfriend had used inside places and a choice of beds, she preferred be out at "our place," where they could listen to the cicadas, down a few beers, skip some stones, talk about stuff, and make out. The "our place" that she and Ryan referred to was just past the low water crossing, where Boos Lane hopped over the Pedernales River. Instead of following the uphill fork to River Road, Ryan's big-block Ford 460 jumped off the low water crossing, ground its way along the stony riverbed, and tucked itself inside a cozy stand of cypress trees just off the bank. With the headlights off, a spray of stars would splash through the windshield and hang above the pastures on the opposite side of the river—the opportune parking spot for young lovers. They had learned how to kiss there. *Really* kiss.

"Seems like we been out of school long enough." Ryan was all looks and simplicity, and he didn't require much effort on Willow's part. He leaned back in the driver's seat, his foot up on the dashboard, a longneck Lone Star beer in his hand. While talking to Willow in the seat next to him, his eyes were fixed straight ahead, like he was still driving. "Now we got all settled into a regular paycheck, and ya notice how our old running buddies been dropping one by one, getting married, getting started with their families. And I've been wondering what you were thinkin'."

The radio was on, and Gary P. Nunn was crooning out into the night over the tinny truck speakers.

"Me?" Willow, too, was just looking out at the stars. "I was wondering when you were going to get around to fixing those speakers."

She noticed that he wore a clean shirt and wasn't dipping that night, a clear indication of his amorous intentions. She was leaning back against the passenger door when he moved in on her, sliding his arm over her shoulders and pulling himself onto her. She moved the beer from between her legs to the dashboard and willingly took his kiss. They were twisted in an awkward and familiar position in the front seat of the truck, and she was expecting him to unbutton her blouse, but instead he unsnapped his breast pocket and retrieved a small, velvet-covered box that had *Segner's Jewelers ~ 997-6524* printed in silver script on the lid.

Ryan popped it open with his thumb. Willow sat up, drawing in a deep breath, her eyes fixed on the shiny band of silver. Then came his proposal: "You and me, babe. How about it?"

Willow flushed, just as frightened as she was enthralled. "What'd you go and do this for?" She didn't take the box from him.

He shimmied in closer to her, the pressure of his body holding her in place. "Here, let me show you how it works." He began to ease the ring onto her finger. "It's a kinda simple piece of equipment. Works kinda like this." He applied a bit more force. "And when properly inserted, it works for your whole life."

"It's kinda tight." She kept her finger just slightly bent. "It's not going all the way on."

He grinned into her eyes, and then brought himself even more fully on top of her. Now she felt trapped, but she responded to his deep kiss by offering a little tongue of her own.

When his free hand started to work at the snap on her jeans, she whispered, "I can't let you do that."

"Do what, little darlin'?"

"I'm on my period now," she lied.

"Rain check, then." Ryan pulled himself off of her, and they both sat back in their respective seats. He held her hand up to let the moon reflect off the ring, still stuck just past her first knuckle, not all the way on. "So now, when do you want to get married, then?"

"This is so much to digest at one time, Ryan. I'm gonna have to talk to my mom."

"Big wedding, little wedding, I don't care. I just want to see you raising a lot of little kids that look just like me and just like you all at the same time."

Images of that future rattled through her head on the drive back into town: snapshots of swing sets and toddlers in diapers running in the yard, pulling on her skirts, her very own husband smiling from the porch—the porch of the same house that she lived in now. *This could be it.* All the way home she fiddled with the ring that was stuck on her first knuckle, not wanting him to think she was trying to take it off. A good-night kiss at her mom's house sent Ryan off to the South Star to take high fives from his buddies and have a last dance with some old girlfriends. That's the way it went down in Fredericksburg.

The air was stale and the house was quiet. Her mom was still out, and Willow drifted to the linen closet looking for some clean towels. There she found a package of single-edge utility blades with only one missing, the one her mother had probably used to start a project before forgetting where she had left the package. Willow wrapped a towel around her neck, pulled one blade out of the box, and carried it with her to the stuffed chair by the window in the living room.

She took a moment to study the ring. It was simple, and she could see that Ryan had spent more than he could afford on it. *This could be it,* she thought again—the very thing that would nail down a future here in Fredericksburg. Up to this point in her life, she just took the next step along a path that had been laid out for her, like her mother had done. Now she actually had to do something of her own volition. She felt that burden keenly as she flicked the engagement ring into the ashtray on the end table, switched on the lamp, and bent over to stare into the palm of her left hand as if she were trying to read her own fortune.

With familiar precision she cut a diagonal line between the first knuckle and the base of her ring finger. The skin was firm there, and blood started squirting as soon as the blade broke the surface. Drops of red fell onto her blouse.

"Dang!" she cried out, recoiling. *Didn't expect that.*

Pursing her lips and refocusing like a determined artisan, she leaned in to create a pattern. Carefully placing the tip of the razor at the bottom of the first cut, she hesitated, then forced herself to make a quick upward slice, a bit deeper than the first, leaving a *V* shape oozing blood into her palm. The flesh was tough or the blade was dull, challenging her skill, but Willow remained determined and pressed on with yet another diagonal cut that, again, was too deep. Then she laid back a flap of skin that peeled away from her finger.

This time there was no secret whisper, nothing of the euphoria that Willow had experienced at one time. It stung. Badly. And blood trickled through the concave bowl of her hand. *Why so much?* she thought, holding her hand before her face, watching the red rivulets seek out the creases of her palm. This innate habit of hers had become more of a project—something she did rather than something she felt. Abruptly, she tossed the blade into the ashtray with her new ring. Somehow she wanted to cry, but found she was no longer that kind of person. She had grown hard, like the Texas limestone, and besides, she was making a mess all over her mother's towel.

• • •

Relying more on the alcohol than on his charm, Brady convinced Thea to follow him from the wine bar to his house. He had promised her some of his private stash of mesquite-roasted coffee, "the most awesome coffee you'll ever drink. One cup will erase a hangover."

Brady's kids were wrapped up in blankets and crashed out in the blue glow of the television, with pizza crusts and open bags of chips littering the floor around them.

"This is Miguel," he said as he hefted the smallest off the sofa and over his shoulder. "He's the lightest."

Brady carried him down the hall and came back for the one who was curled up on the floor, a mop of hair in her face. "Margit, sweetie."

The girl raised her head and squinted around the room. She looked at her dad and lay her head down again.

"Come on, sweetie. Let's get our teeth brushed."

When Margit got to her feet, she stared for a moment at Thea and said, "You mean *my* teeth."

"Yes. Your teeth." With her dad's support she teetered down the hall like a newborn lamb.

"Hey, you did a good job tonight, watching your brother and taking care of the house," Brady was telling her as they turned into the bathroom.

He came back to Thea a few minutes later with a smile of accomplishment. "Let's get that coffee going." He ushered her into the kitchen.

"You going to put me to bed, too?" Thea asked as she dropped herself into a chair at his kitchen table.

"I aim to," Brady said, pulling a pair of mugs off the shelf. "But let's give the kids a chance to fall into a really deep sleep."

The ring of Brady's cell phone startled them both. In unison, they turned their heads to the kitchen clock. A second ring. Late-night calls were inevitably bad-news calls. Brady stepped into the hallway with his phone. He returned quickly and reported to Thea in a particularly curt manner: "I have to fetch someone out at the South Star."

Thea followed Brady uninvited to his daughter's bedroom, where he sat on the bed next to Margit. He rubbed her belly until her eyes flickered open. "Hey, Tinkerbell." When the girl looked up at her father, he said, "I have to run out for just a few minutes."

Margit grunted and turned her face to her pillow.

"I'll be back very quickly. I just have to pick someone up."

Her eyes fell shut and she shook her head, more to be left alone than in acknowledgment.

"I know you'll be okay, but if your brother gets up, just bring him in bed with you. Okay?"

She nodded this time, trying to get back to sleep.

Brady stood and tucked his shirt into his jeans. Thea, watching from just outside the bedroom door, felt more bewildered than angry. Brady put his hand on her arm and said in a quiet voice, almost a whisper, "Mari's down at the South Star. I've got to fetch her. Shouldn't take too long."

"Was that her who called just now?"

"No. It was Gina, the bartender."

"So you're the Fredericksburg after-hours taxi service?"

He might have laughed at a comment like that, but instead he replied with a stern glare. "Something like that." On the way out the front door, he left Thea with an ambiguous choice of words, as though he had no idea what to do with her: "The kids are all right. I'll be back real quick."

•   •   •

All he had to do was get to the South Star and back. Thursday, Friday, and Saturday night, for as long as Brady could remember, the dateless and the desperate had the choice of going to the South Star out on the San Antonio highway or to a cowboy dive down by the stockyards that changed its name every other year. It now carried the moniker of Das Roadhaus, Ja. Their great attraction was "Bo and His Band," which played Country Top 40, and the mixed drinks served until 2 a.m.

Brady's familiarity with the honky-tonk came back in the first musty blend of beer and cigarette smoke that greeted him at the door. It was dark inside and dense with mirthful bodies pressed shoulder to shoulder, neon bar lights silhouetting their hair and hats. Noise from the band and voices trying to shout over the band pounded off every wall, and there at the bar was Jeanie Geische, plastered.

"Yo, Brady." She grabbed at him from her stool and shouted in his ear, "Everything is cool with the fair."

He gave her a lost, inquisitive look and a shrug. Words were so hard in here.

"I got it now," she yelled, clutching at his shirt. "I'm going with my brother."

"Gerdie here?" he shouted back to her.

"What?"

"Where is Gerdie?"

"Didn't come . . ." She said something else that Brady couldn't understand.

"Where is Mari?"

She gave him an ugly look and bellowed, "I couldn't give a shit about her." Then she pointed toward the restrooms.

Brady elbowed his way through the dense and fetid crowd before he found Mari holding herself upright, just inside the door of the ladies' bathroom. She was going neither in nor out—just holding on. Brady stepped in and grabbed her under the arms while two girls with fresh makeup and bloodshot eyes shoved their way past him.

"Use your own," one of them hollered. Then they looked at each other and laughed.

Mari's face was painted in a listless expression. Her head rolled around her shoulders, down to her chin, then snapped back up as if she'd suddenly awoken. When she started slithering to the floor, Brady grabbed her. She seemed to recognize Brady, but she pushed away, slurring something like, "I'm okay. Okay!"

As she pulled away from him, she crashed hard into the back of some bad-looking dude with a black cowboy hat. When the cowboy turned to meet his assailant, Mari belched right onto his chest, depositing a disgusting glob of yellow drool on his black cowboy shirt.

"Goddamn!" the man sung out over the din. "That bitch puked on me."

Brady grabbed Mari's arm from behind as she reeled backwards.

Girls nearby went, "Ewww," and the cowboy's friends stepped up, belligerent and eager for trouble.

Brady jostled Mari into a more maneuverable position and held his hand up. His words, "Keep it cool," were heard by no one.

From the dark cacophony of bodies pressed around them, young Ryan Ebberhaus pushed his way onto the scene. He seemed to be buzzing, and a couple of his friends followed him into the fray, which drew up the fight lines, if there was going to be one. The music and the background noise were still loud enough to drown out anything that could be said between them.

There was sawdust in Mari's hair. Her stomach convulsed again, and her eyes rolled. Brady held her head upright and told her, "Time to go, babe."

Mari made an effort to muster some resistance, but Brady held her firmly, scooping her into his arms in one gorilla-like move, and followed Ryan as he bulled a path to the door. The music slowed to a country waltz, while the uproarious crowd kept the deafening babble. As they started to push their way out, Brady heard the man in the black cowboy hat hollering after them, "Yeah, you moron. Get that drunken whore out of here."

The guys around him let out a roar of laughter louder than the band. Brady seethed, encumbered by the embarrassment of Mari's limp body. He was mad at her, but his ire was focused on the loudmouth in the black hat and the newly stained shirt. Blocked by the density of the crowd ahead, Ryan turned, and Brady just dropped the limp Mari into his arms, cocked his elbow, and threw his right fist into the shirt-stained cowboy's face. Arms out and stunned like a slaughterhouse cow, the man stumbled backwards into the edge of a table and crashed to the floor, taking chairs, glasses, and bottles down with him.

The music came to an immediate halt on that one single beat. The leather-vested band leader, a man they all knew as

Bo—just Bo—took just a moment to set his Fender Stratocaster into its guitar stand, took one long step off the band platform, and pushed his way across the dance floor, gracelessly parting the seas of kickers and sweethearts as he plowed into the scene.

He quickly stepped between the two of them, addressing the cowboy first. "You okay?" Then he drilled his eyes into Brady. "Get her out of here, Brady. Now."

Brady and Ryan, who still had Mari draped in his arms, had no trouble making it to the door.

Jeanie, still on her barstool, held her glass up as they made the door. "Dang, Brady. You sure know how to pick up a girl."

As soon as the door slammed behind them, Bo had his guitar slung over his shoulder and the joint was rocking again.

• • •

Brady pulled up to his house in the quiet darkness of the long night. He found Thea sitting at the kitchen table with a cup of mesquite-roasted coffee in her hands.

"Still here? Still up?" he asked as he came in.

"Just waiting." She paused, offended at his greeting. "But I'm sober now, and there's no headache."

Brady sat down across the table from Thea and studied her for a moment. She didn't look angry and she didn't say a thing.

"It's complicated," he said at last.

Instead of responding, Thea got up, poured out a fresh cup of coffee, and brought it to him, saying, "Your coffee's terrible."

"It's like I'm her big brother or something. Bad sister." He could see that Thea wasn't buying it, and he bit down against the anger rising from every direction. "Promised my brother that I would look after her while he was away." It bothered him that she was just sitting there, mute. "He was going to marry her when he got back." Brady wiped at his eyes. "Never figured he'd be gone forever. So?"

"Do you think that's what Gus would have done?"

It was the tone in her voice that irked him. He knew that he had put her in an awkward position, but if she had meant that as an insult, it was out of line. "She wouldn't be out there if Gus was here," he mumbled before moving to a new topic. "I'm surprised to find you still here."

"Did you think I'd go home?"

He nodded and confessed, "I did." He was flattered she was here, but at the same time uncomfortable about why she had stayed.

"Did you think that I would run out just like that? Like everyone else running off on poor Brady?" Her words had a caustic tone. "You thrive on that, don't you?"

"On what?" He found the growing hostility in her eyes unnerving.

"I know what's going on with you. I know why you get up in the middle of the night to drag drunks out of bars. It's the same reason that you pull helpless orphans out of Mexico and Bolivia."

"Peru."

"What?"

"Margit's from Peru, not Bolivia," he corrected. Thea just sat there staring at him. After a long pause Brady mansplained, "Bolivia is further south. It's more multiethnic than Peru."

"Peru, then," she conceded, but pressed her point. "When did it become your mission to save the world, one drunk at a time?"

"What are you getting at, Thea?"

She paused. "How old were you when your mom and dad died?"

His hackles were up. "What is this? One of your Austin

group therapy sessions? All that is a long time behind me now. It's nothing to you. Or me."

"Is it really, Brady? Or do you just keep playing it over and over again?" She raised her coffee to her lips, keeping her eyes on him as she sipped. When she finished, she continued pressing her thesis. "Do you know what I have always admired about you, Brady? You've always pulled yourself through. You had some tough stuff thrown at you. But you always pull through." She hesitated a bit. "Your heart is as big as it is stupid."

That might have been some kind of compliment or it might have been an insult, but Brady didn't want to sort that out. "Don't go there, Thea." He held his hand up to stop her.

She didn't stop. "The way you deal with other people is just weird. Rescuing Margit from poverty in"—she added a satirical emphasis—"Peru."

Brady nodded. She got that one right.

"Then Miguel. And rescuing Mari Hilss from her tragic life at the South Star. None of that's going to help them."

"Help who?" Brady asked.

Thea leaned over the table, with the coffee cup directly under her chin. "The dead ones. The ones who abandoned you."

Brady sat back. To him she looked like a witch casting a spell.

"None of this is going to help them." Thea pointed down the hall to the rooms where Margit and Miguel slept. "If that is what you are trying to do."

Brady was shaking his head, straining to keep his anger checked. "I've seen a lot of people just turn away, Thea. Change their mind about the promises they made or how they feel. Pretend they can't do anything. You may be right, and maybe I do things for all the wrong reasons. Maybe you can choose not to get tangled up with people who might become a burden to you. But that's not what I am, and if that's the way you are, this isn't going to work. You and me."

"Work? What?" She stood, almost slapping the table, gasping for breath and grabbing for words. "What do you think this is? You don't. Oh, God." She turned away, scolding herself out loud. "What a mistake." Then, spinning back toward Brady: "Don't you make more of this than it was." She stomped off to the living room, where she had left her small leather purse and her car keys.

Brady kept his seat at the kitchen table and felt the aftershock of his front door slamming. He had blown that one, and he couldn't help but think that it was all Mari's fault.

He rose up and went to sit next to the sleeping Margit, where he watched her slowly pull air into her little body and easily let it out again. He slowly moved the back of his finger around her smooth cheek and brushed the wayward strands of hair from her lips. "I'm sorry, little angel," he said aloud. Privately, he had once thought himself something of a hero for adopting these children from the Lutheran Charities, but now he wondered who was rescuing whom.

Margit stirred, rolled her head, and flickered her eyes awake. Her deep brown eyes looked into his, then past him. Brady turned to see where she was looking.

Thea stood in the bedroom door.

He hadn't heard her return, and for a moment, just a brief moment, he felt his body drained of blood, thinking that she may have come back to him. Or maybe Thea had been quiet out of respect for the tender moment, the kind of moment she had never known as a child.

"You have to move your car," she said in a soft tone. "You're blocking me in."

The Last Road Trip
of Max Ritzi

There is nothing that rouses the vigor of expired youth like the passing blur of a highway, elbow out the window, radio loud, warm breeze ruffling through thinning hair while the scenic grandeur of the American Southwest rolls past, like you're riding a wave. Max Ritzi was squarely in his middle age, but the view through the windshield brought with it a grin of youthful promise. That future was disrupted by an occasional glance into the rearview mirror and the reminder that this trip marked the end of his second marriage. He was leaving his wife, leaving her daughter, and leaving Arizona pretty much the way he came in—rambling around in a car, looking for work. Behind his road trip smile, he found it hard to admit that after she threw him out, he had no place left to go but back to Fredericksburg.

Nevertheless, he was coming home in a pitch-black Dodge Challenger, a badge of his success that harkened back to the muscle car fantasies of his youth. It was that success that drove the final wedge between him and his soon-to-be ex-wife, Caroline. In a career that transitioned like flip cards, from construction to warehouse work and selling building materials, Max had stumbled into a multilevel marketing scheme that sold an energy booster called the Power Patch.

Billed as an alternative to protein shakes and energy drinks, the Power Patch worked like those quit-smoking stick-on strips and found a cult following among gym rats and fitness geeks. He cultivated a talent for selling bulk quantities of this "vitamin voodoo," as Caroline called it, to amateur athletic groups, and for taking in money from downline distributors. The gulf between Max and his wife grew in earnest when Max left his day job to pursue the Power Patch as a full-time career.

"It's a total scam that appeals to the sleazeball side of your personality," Caroline scolded, and after Max attempted to recruit members of her own family, she went ballistic. Of course, the Power Patch was merely the most recent flashpoint in their already broken marriage, and to Max it was a convenient excuse to move on.

"I'll be cruising back home in this two-door, hardtop classic coupe, paid for in cash," he argued as he drove. "That'll show my old hometown buddies what you get for getting out in the world. All thanks to the vitamin voodoo. And when I get home, I'm going to really shake it up. Make myself some real train-riding money."

Keeping with his newly affluent self-image, Max checked into a Zagat-rated hotel in the center of Santa Fe and spent the night at the rooftop bar, taste-testing his way through their menu of margaritas. When he ordered his first tequila shot, he borrowed a pen from the bartender so he could make a list on his cocktail napkin: things to do when he got back home. But he got distracted by an olive-skinned lady with hair that fell like feathers over her naked shoulders. She was whooping it up with her friends at the loudest table on the roof—reminding him of someone he might add to his cocktail napkin list. He scribbled it down: *The one that got away.*

"Mari Hilss," he whispered to his shot glass. The girl he might have married. *Should have stuck with the script,* he thought. *Stayed in town, had some kids right away, worked my dad's place until I was fat and boring.*

He downed his tequila in one quick gulp and slammed the empty glass on the bar. "Yeah, but Carel screwed that up for me," he said, loud enough to get the bartender's attention.

"Ready for another, *amigo?*"

Max pointed to his empty shot glass. "Hit me again." He picked up the pen and added another line to his to-do list: *Kick Carel's ass.*

It was the hotel housekeeper who rousted Max out of bed the next day, past checkout time and a night of tequila still pounding in his head. There was nothing for him to do in Santa Fe but get a plate of *migas* and find his car. The open road helped ease his headache. Pushing around the southern horn of the Sangre de Cristo Mountains—where the final run of the mighty Rockies collapses into the great Chihuahuan Desert—Max pierced through a hot August afternoon of crusty pueblos and cottonwood bottoms at speeds as high as the temperature outside. Then, after a long couple of hours behind the wheel, he crossed the Texas line and was swallowed by an endless flat of sagebrush and bad memories.

Not a rock had moved, not a shrub had grown, it seemed, since Max had first crossed the Llano Estacado decades earlier. Back then he was an outlaw on the run in a pieced-together, unregistered, uninsured, and mostly baby blue Camaro with one banged-up gray door that was kept closed with a twist of bailing wire. That beat-up car could have broken down out there; he could have ended up with turkey buzzards standing on his chest. He'd actually had that dream, over and over again. This was the place of that recurring nightmare.

Things were bad for him in Fredericksburg when he'd left. His maniacal father had been ready to kill him. Actually kill him. But Max was at the top of his game now, making money and cruising home like he owned the road.

By the time he reached Sweetwater, the sun was down but there was still light in the sky. The moon sat like an immense kumquat on the horizon. The road was still hot, and the moaning in his stomach reminded him of the microwaved burrito he had picked up at a Texaco station outside of Lubbock. At this speed he'd be back in Gillespie County well before midnight. The two-lane West Texas highway kept rolling into his headlights and falling under his wheels. The nearer those roads drew him to Fredericksburg, the more frequently his thoughts turned to his father.

Out of that unending blacktop came composite images of those terrible family suppers: his father standing up from his chair, a napkin still dangling from his neck, red-faced and leaning halfway across the table, one hand drawn up into a fist, ready to strike. He was always yelling, pointing, and threatening. Max could envision his sister, Gerdie, breaking into tears, and his little brother, Jock, stuttering out rapid apologies for something that had nothing to do with him. This was the vivid and recurring image of his childhood. Max wondered now if it was all an exaggerated memory that he had nurtured in his own head over so many years away.

He was ready to see his father again. Now a man standing on his own, Max didn't have to put up with the belittling and the yelling that had defined his childhood. And as cruel as the old man could be, he was in a wheelchair now. If it came to blows, Max could take him.

• • •

Ba-wham! The Challenger jumped. In the road. Off the road. Screeching. Animal? Tires? And a bump. A hard bump. The fender, up and over . . . something. Headlights panned the desert brush, and another . . . thump—back wheels this time. A dog-sized mass skidded across the pavement, and a swatch of wet darkness smeared the road.

Max worked the wheel with tight knuckles and reached for a prayer he'd long forgotten. He kept his foot off the brake and pulled the car out of the skid. The headlights had just started to find the white lane lines, when with one final, jarring blow— *What was that?*—the car came to a hard stop, and Max's forehead ricocheted off the steering wheel. Everything stopped. A fine dust trickled down about him, or so it seemed.

Dead silence.

A slow pain welling up across his forehead pulled Max from a fog. He squeezed his eyes tightly. That made him nauseous. Slowly he reached for the car door and stepped out into the night. Good—he could stand. Overhead, stars undulated and the moon, fully round and yellow now, moved in and out of focus. Sweetwater was somewhere back there, but he couldn't remember what the next town was. The loudest sound in the night was the pounding of his own heart.

After checking to see how solid the earth was under his feet, and without a flashlight, Max tiptoed toward the dark mass heaped on the pavement. He saw no movement except the steady flow of blood oozing from mouth and anus. The bristled hair of a wild boar, much bigger than a large dog, lay cleaved with long gashes where its hide had been torn away. Behind a gnarled tusk, one open eye reflected the moon.

The saliva glands in Max's mouth told him that he was about to vomit.

He hurried back to his car, gulping in the dry night air, but he kept that Texaco burrito in his stomach. The driver's-side headlight had been shattered and its housing smashed, while the one good light shot its cone out into the vast nothingness of West Texas. The front bumper was stove in, the fender panel mashed up. The motor was still running. He reached in and turned it off.

He didn't want to, but Max returned to the corpse and just stood over it wondering where the beast had been headed. Home to rejoin *his* family, perhaps? That hog had a father too—a daughter, maybe.

Just get it out of the highway, Max instructed himself. Taking a deep breath, he took hold of the bristly forelegs and heaved on them. The mass didn't yield, but a hot stream of blood shot up from an open artery, catching Max just below his neck and splashing up onto his chin.

"Oh, God. Holy shit." Max danced around, chanting profanities. Again, this would have been a good time to puke, but his stomach just convulsed and nothing came to his throat.

Max removed his belt and looped it around the neck of the beast. With a lot of tugging and rolling, he lugged it off the road and then a little bit further, and with a push, let the mangled pig roll into a shallow arroyo. Max pulled off his shirt—now drenched in sweat and blood. He tossed it down on top of the dead animal, imagining the turkey buzzards that would soon be feasting on it.

Regaining himself, Max found his tire iron and mustered

the strength to pry the stove-in fender away from the front tire. He used a rock to shape the headlight housing back against the hood. Reaching into the trunk, he rummaged through his duffel bag for a clean T-shirt. Then, back behind the wheel, he turned the key and moved the car down the road at a more cautious speed. Now he'd be coming back to Fredericksburg the way he'd left—pretty much a wreck.

There was more highway that night, and lots more emptiness to cross before the low mesquite plains gave way to oak stands, undulating hills, and dry river beds. Where the old Mason Highway crested near the Hilltop Café, the first lights of Fredericksburg scraped against the night sky, and Max turned off onto an unmarked farm-to-market road. As he reentered the gravitational pull of his childhood, the bends and turns of these back roads came to him instinctively. He'd learned to drive out here. He'd started drinking and smooching on girls out here. He'd hidden from his father out here.

It was a Saturday night, and he'd been told that his old gang would be out at the party ranch. His once glorious muscle car scraped bottom as he edged it down the caliche roads that cut across fields of dried-up coastal hay, through the pecan groves, and up toward the ranch house of Aubrey and Adelheid Weshausen.

"Addy'll make up a room for you, Max. You're always welcome here if it gets too hot at your old man's house," Aubrey had told him before he left Flagstaff. "Gerdie told me she's moving her kids out of your old room for your visit. But I know how it can get. They still don't use an air conditioner."

Max nodded. "Might take you up on that."

Max and Aubrey were friends from childhood. Max had taken Addy out on her first date. Max and Aubrey played four years of high school football together. And when Max made his escape from Texas, it was in Aubrey's baby blue Camaro with one gray door.

Several pickup trucks were spaced haphazardly across the lawn area between the Weshausens' ranch house and the barn. The house lights shone, and music seeped out of open windows. Between the barn and the creek, a solemn group of shadows stood about the low-burning embers of a bonfire. Max got out of his car and stepped stiffly over to join the silhouettes at the fire.

They were stoned in their places with long-necked beer bottles in their hands, making conversation out of ambiguities like *Yeah, man* and *Fuck that*. With the dying fire reflecting off their faces, Max picked them out one by one as he approached: Heinie Ortner, Rickie Boensch, Buddy Nuweinkraus—guys who had made up the better part of the offensive line on Max's football team. Bonded for life, they now stood exactly where Max had last seen them ten, fifteen years ago: standing around a campfire, drinking beer.

Not one of them seemed surprised to see Max just mosey up to the fire. It was as if they had been totally expecting their long-lost wide receiver to appear.

"Hey, Buddy," Max greeted his old friend.

Buddy nodded, keeping his eyes on the diminishing fire as if shifting his gaze would make him fall over.

"Rickie. You been keeping okay?"

Rickie Boensch looked at Max a minute, working to put something together in his head. Then he spoke. "Hey. Get yourself a beer, man."

Max stuck his hand in a washtub of melted ice and felt around for a bottle. Heinie was squinting at him, his eyes rolling under the brim of that black cowboy hat as though trying to recognize him.

"Hey, Road Trip," Heinie said at last, using Max's old nickname. "Where'd you get that fuckin' lump on your head?"

• • •

After one and a half days of driving, three states, two time zones, and four of America's geological regions—and after waking up with a hangover for a second day in a row—Max faced the most grueling part of that journey: the last twenty-three miles down old Tivydale Road, to town and his father's house.

Tivydale Road rolled indolently through small stands of live oak trees and long pastures beaten yellow by the relentless sun. Peach orchards ebbed and flowed over the swells of land, their meticulous rows tied together with the black hoses of drip irrigation. Recently sheared sheep lay in the dust around water tanks, eking out what shade they could and grazing the shrub lines along the fences. Then the road just came to an end.

At State Highway 16 the town of Fredericksburg began in earnest with its first traffic signal. At that crossroad the hulking grandstands loomed over the empty show barns and the pari-mutuel racetrack of the Gillespie County Fairgrounds, home of the oldest county fair in the state. The signal light changed to green and Max Ritzi made a left turn, smack into the jaws of his Lutheran childhood.

Before he could knock, his mother burst through the door, her heart in her voice: "Oh, *mein kleiner* Max, it's so good to . . . Whatever happened to your head?" Then, feigning a scolding tone, she said, "You've been out with those roughnecks again."

"It's just a—"

"You had better let Gerdie take a look at that."

"Is Gerdie here?" he asked as his mama pulled him inside the house.

"*Ja. Ja.* She's here with *opa*."

Maximilian Ritzi, the *opa* himself, stood gaunt and stiff in the far corner of the room, propped up by his daughter on one side and an aluminum cane on the other. He was swallowed up in his loose clothes: his faded canvas shirt buttoned at the neck and a leather belt that could have gone around him twice. When Gerdie stepped out to greet her brother, her smile radiant, the old man teetered a bit and she moved back to shore him up.

Inside it was a different kind of hot, reminding Max that the old house had but one window air conditioner that they used sparingly.

"You gonna shut dat door, boy? Let all dem flies come in here?" The old man's voice had not lost its vigor.

Max was caught momentarily between a greeting and an answer to his father's question when Maximilian fired again. "What dat dere you got on yer head, boy?"

Checking himself against his father's rancor, Max put on a smile and crossed the room.

"You come in here and sit a spell." The old man pointed his cane at the sofa in a gesture that tipped him off balance. Gerdie tightened her grip, but Maximilian fended her off by slapping at her with his free hand.

Rather than follow his father's direction, Max stepped up to him and wrapped his arms around the old man's shoulders. He felt the old man's clammy skin and protruding bones. This close, Max could smell the chewed-up cigars that stained his teeth, and he took note of the ashtrays where the old man usually sat. His Bible was there too, thick and well worn.

Tucked partially behind the well-worn La-Z-Boy chair was an oxygen converter the size of a woodstove, and plastic tubes draped the arm of the chair, softly hissing. His father had made a great effort to be standing on his own feet when he greeted his son.

The two men broke away and took their respective seats, squaring off across from each other. Evelyn Ritzi, ever the good *hausfrau*, scurried off to fetch them some iced tea. Gerdie, grinning like a girl on her first date, took a seat on the sofa, close enough to Max to be flirting.

"So, your wife couldn't make it here now." The old man spoke with an effort. "Has she some kind of problem?"

"No. No problem. And her name is Caroline."

"*Ja, ja.* I know dat. Caroline. My Mexican daughter-in-law."

Mexican. Already the old man was throwing insults. Max cheerfully blurted back, "She wanted to come, but she couldn't get off of work." Immediately he saw that his father knew he was lying.

Maximilian cleared his throat and with a slow and deliberate movement laid his big right hand on the Bible as if he were taking an oath.

Gerdie was showing some concern and started to push herself up. "*Opa,* I think you need some—"

"*Nay!*" Their father barked harshly enough to push Gerdie back into her seat.

Evelyn rejoined them with a tray of clinking iced-tea glasses. "It's so wonderful to have you home, Max. This year we'll have the whole family together at the fair."

"*Ach,* ya never know where dis boy's been off to," bawled the old man, drawing all the attention back upon himself. His head was bouncing up and down as if he'd made a joke. "Not a thought to his own family."

Max allowed a moment of silence to pass but spoke up before his father could continue. "It's good to see you again, Papa."

His mother intervened with a different subject. "Well, dear. Your old bedroom is ready for you."

"Oh, Mama, Aubrey invited me to stay with him at the ranch. I don't want to throw the kids out of their room."

"Aubrey Weshausen!" The patriarch jumped back into the conversation. "Now dere's a boy who made a no-good mess wit' his father's ranch, dere. One time de finest Dorpers in de county came off dat ranch. But no more, *ich sage dir*."

That statement settled over them like a fog. Max didn't feel it necessary to answer. So Maximilian drew in a breath— almost a snore—and continued.

"An' my boy wanna be doin' more hard drinkin' and carousin' about wit' de old line out dere at Aubrey Weshausen's ranch. Would ya not? Rather dan choosing to be wit' de Christian family dat you were born into?"

"Hard drinking, Papa? I gave up hard drinking years ago. I'm just a beer man now." It was his second lie.

"*Ja.*" The old man scratched his chin and pretended to think about that. "Now dat musta been when you got hitched up to dat Mexican girl? One we never got to meet."

"Her name is Caroline, Papa. And you did meet her when I was out for . . ." He turned to Gerdie. "Was that when you were moving back in here?"

"Yes, it was." Gerdie was wringing her hands and bobbing her head like she was in trouble. "Yes. You and Caroline did come back and help us with that move. I liked her. She was sweet."

It hurt Max, seeing his older sister still quaking in the shadow of their father. "I recall that you didn't take kindly to your Mexican daughter-in-law." He turned away from his father to engage his mother and sister. "Caroline is the one who had me give up the 'heavy drinking and carousing,' as you call it."

His mother smiled for him to continue.

"When Caroline took up yoga, she told me that there was no room for that kind of karma in our home."

"I think you have a very smart wife, Max." His mother beamed even more pleasantly. "I have never known wherever you would put a karma in a home."

"In any case," Gerdie jumped in, "the kids have already moved into my room, and they are eager to spend some time with their Uncle Max. Besides, the TV is in my room, so this will be a treat for them."

"Okay, then," Max agreed, believing he'd done well with his father and feeling unable to deny his mother's hopeful smile. "I'll have to pick up a toothbrush and a razor. I left mine at the ranch," he said, to let them know that he was keeping his options open.

A snort from Maximilian took their attention. His head had dropped to one side, and a little line of dribble traced his chin. His lips had taken on a blue cast.

Gerdie wiped his lips in a way that wouldn't wake him. She pulled the plastic tubing that hissed with oxygen and gently placed it under his nose. "It's time for a rest. There has been a lot of excitement for him this morning." She turned to Max with a look that said everything was all right.

In his view, it wasn't.

• • •

The neighborhood settled in the hush of a torrid August afternoon. The small house's large yard was shaded by one-hundred-year-old pecan trees bent heavy over a rusted-out mechanical harvester that Maximilian was going to neither repair nor get rid of. With evening, the scrubby hills lost their harsh edges and the long, red-streaked sunset overtook the landscape. Mockingbirds and grackles picked themselves out of the trees and flocked across the sky to their night roosts out west.

Max sat in the backyard shade, paging through a week-old edition of the *Fredericksburg Standard Radio-Post*. The scent of honeysuckle mingled with the odd tang of sauerkraut that seeped out of the kitchen, where his mother and sister were sweating over supper. He didn't know where his father was being kept, and he didn't plan on looking.

All at once a great commotion exploded inside the house, as if a hamster cage had been tipped over. Children in a wide range of sizes—all blond-haired, blue-eyed Ritzi kids—scurried throughout the house looking for their Uncle Max. Two of them were Gerdie's, and four were their cousins, Jock's kids— the sum total of Max's nieces and nephews.

Max's younger brother, Jock—who, by an odd twist, had never played sports (the nickname was for Jochiem)—came bouncing out of the back door. "Hey, big brother. I saw your, uh, car. What hap-happened . . ." He stopped mid-stutter when Max stood to greet him. "Wha . . . what happened to your head?"

"Brain tumor. Didn't Mama tell you?" They ruffled each other's hair, commented on their receding hairlines, traded jabs, and threw their arms around each other.

"It's not . . . not contagious, is it?" Jock joked.

"Not contagious, little brother. But it's known to be hereditary."

They laughed together as the backyard was suddenly filled with the running, squealing children who had been shooed out of the house. Each, in turn, ran up and bounced a quick hug off the curious Uncle Max. Terri, Jock's perpetually overwhelmed wife, followed behind the children, guiding and refereeing them like a teacher in a schoolyard.

The one thing Max always missed about his home were those capacious family suppers set out on that long plank, a make-shift dinner table under the shade of those ancient pecan trees. Christmas, Easter, Fourth of July, Gillespie County Fair . . . it was always roast pork, Mama's home-fermented sauerkraut, red potato salad, and beer. In former times it had been home-made beer, but that was one of the things that Maximilian had had to give up and his youngest son wouldn't take up.

When everyone was in their place around the plank table, Maximilian, refreshed from an extended, oxygenated nap, gave the blessing. It was a long and serious one—as Lutherans were wont to give—that didn't leave much out. Then the food was passed. They ate, gabbed, laughed, and basked in the warmth of family.

After dinner, while the women cleaned up and the nieces and nephews ran off to climb into the corners of the big back-yard, the men sat around to talk about livestock prices, farm equipment, and other topics that didn't require them to engage their emotions.

Maximilian worked a cigar from its cellophane wrapper with a shaking hand. He didn't smoke them anymore; rather he sucked on the end and rolled it in his mouth until it was soggy. Jock, who was now running the family business, brought out some photos: glossy color pictures of late-model trucks with brush guards and custom bumper rails.

"This the kind of work you've been turning out at the shop?" Max asked.

"No. No. It's been the kind of thing we've been thinking

about doing. I mean, we've been . . . Well, we done some." Jock started to explain, in his own hesitant way, how the shop had been fitting brush guards and clearance protection to the designer pickups driven by the weekend ranchers and hunters. "And I think I know where we could get some more. Of this kind of work, I mean."

He laid the photos out on the table before his father, one by one, like he was dealing cards.

"There are, uh, let me see here . . ." Jock fumbled with some brochures, placing them on top of the photos. He never was too good at making his point. "They have these shows, these big conventions for hunters. That's where we could go to get more work like this. It's a . . . well . . . more money in it. Those fancy truck people are richer, for one thing. And we're good at it, and nobody else around here is doing it."

Finding it difficult to follow his brother's line of thought, Max reached toward the table and picked up the brochure that his father refused to touch.

"These hunter shows . . . they have them in, uh, Houston and San Antonio and up in F-F-Fort Worth." Jock struggled against their father's harsh indifference, but forced himself to continue. "They . . . they get some, it says in there, some three hundred thousand hunters. Big-city guys who . . . who come up here to hunt. At their hunting leases. And, well, they have . . . they're the ones with these expensive trucks."

Max and the old man waited.

Maximilian rolled his cigar and spoke. "Dis ain't got nothin' to do wit' anything dat is goin' on in my shop." Then he shouted, "Does it?"

Jock readjusted himself in his seat. "Well, we could. At the shop. Your shop, that is." He avoided his father's eyes but went on in a more sullen tone. "I was just thinking, if we went to these hunter shows—they call them, what, the Hunters Extravaganza shows? We could get more of this kind of business."

With his father's mouth preoccupied with his slobbery cheroot, Max weighed in. "I think it looks like a great idea, little brother." He shoved a brochure at the old man in a way that forced Maximilian to take it in his hand.

They all sat back a moment. Then Maximilian went back to chewing his cigar, and the boys sucked on their beer bottles.

"Well," Jock pleaded, "can I do it?"

Max felt ashamed for his younger brother, asking for permission to run his own business. He glanced at the old man's lap and saw a wrinkled hand clenched in a fist.

Maximilian started wagging his head from side to side, his teeth clamped down on the pulp of his soggy cheroot. "Do what? Go to dis . . . dis Dallas? Dis Houston?" The old man rolled forward in his chair. He slobbered on his chin as his voice grew louder. "You ever bother yourself to ask how much of my money you gonna throw right out on dis?" He took the dirty root of the cigar from his mouth and squashed it into the glossy photos his son had laid out before him, muttering German curses.

His brother effectively silenced, Max stepped up. "Papa," he said in a logical, matter-of-fact tone, "my company pays lots more money than this for trade show booths, and we do that because it brings in hundreds of thousands of dollars in new business. Any business—"

With surprising ferocity, the old man lunged forward in his seat. "Your company? Your company? Ha! Ya don' have no damn company. Since when you know a good day work, even?" Blood rushed into Maximilian's cheeks, and he started to cough and heave.

Max worked to keep a civil tone. "What I know, *opa*, is that you can fill your backyard and your shop with these rusty antiques"—he pointed to shadows in the backyard, where the children were climbing on the old harvester—"but that's not going to keep Ritzi Agricultural Equipment in business long enough to feed those kids. Farming in Gillespie County is dying. Your son has a pretty cool idea on how to keep your business going. And all you can bring yourself to do is trash him."

Jock put a hand up to stop Max. "It's . . . it's okay, Max. That's enough."

A deep grumble came from within Maximilian as he leaned forward, trying to push himself to his feet. "An' whatcha know of farming? Hell, boy, you ever turn a row of God's earth?" There was more bile in him, and he would have brought forth more insults, but he started coughing up phlegm instead.

"What do I know?" Max's voice was rising. "I drove home in a Dodge Challenger coupe, Papa. I know something about making money. And I'm poised to pull down a lot more money than you'll ever pull out of your dying farm equipment shop."

But his father didn't hear him. He had fallen back in his chair, coughing and struggling for breath, his whole body convulsing. Head back, Maximilian tried to suck in air from above them, a mouthful of cigar-stained teeth gasping at the sky, eyes rolling back into their sockets.

Gerdie came running from the kitchen, their mama right behind. She knelt by their father and put a napkin to his mouth. Then she placed an open palm on his chest and turned to Jock. "Bring me his oxygen, *schnell*."

Jock hurried into the house as Maximilian heaved again.

"Just breathe, *opa*. Breathe slowly. Breathe deeply." As the old man calmed down, Gerdie turned to Max with a pained and scolding look. "What did you do, Max? What did you do?"

• • •

Wrapped up tightly in his anger, Carel stepped into Schrubb's office. He had no clever words for the bank folks today. Bev was standing over Schrubb's shoulder, striving to hold her neutral expression. There were no handshakes. No witty greetings. Carel pulled his Resistol from his head, dropped it onto the corner of Schrubb's desk, and plopped himself into his usual chair.

Schrubb's face was glum. "You got our demand letter. Today is the day, so I have to ask. Can you make the payment?"

"Shit, Chuckie," Carel spit back. "Ain't nobody in this damn town got that kind of money just laying around. Unless it be one of your new friends from Houston."

Bev diverted her eyes. Carel imagined that she was getting some visceral satisfaction from this.

Schrubb glanced about his desk, looking for some way out of the inevitable. He rolled his somber expression upward to meet the eyes of his old friend and shrugged. "Then we're going to start with repossession proceeding. I have no way around it, Carel."

Bev passed Schrubb a file folder, which he opened and studied for a moment. "All the construction equipment, including your truck. That lot out on Orchard Street. Your accounts with our bank—we'll close them and claim the balances." He spoke without raising his head. "I was actually surprised to see how much of your property the bank has title to now. Your office, for instance. We already own that, and it looks like you never paid your rent."

Carel nodded quietly. "I knew that."

Schrubb looked up. "What I don't see in here, Carel, is your current residence up on Saddle Drive."

Carel nodded.

"But what we do have is the old Hilss homestead on Washington Street. The house where your ex-wife lives."

"And my daughter." There was a fight brewing in Carel's eyes. "What are you going to do, Chuckie? You going to evict them? How could you!"

Schrubb lunged across the table, yelling now. "I didn't do this, Carel. You did!"

The move startled Carel, who recoiled in his chair. Bev stepped forward but said nothing. Schrubb swallowed loud enough for all to hear and then sat back in his chair.

Carel's cell phone rang. It was Mari. "What do you want?" he answered it.

Bev rolled her eyes and turned away, her words falling away under her breath. "I can't believe . . ."

Carel leaned back in his chair and continued his phone conversation. "And you're just telling me now? . . . At the bank." He paused and then added, "With Schrubb and Bev."

At that, Beverly charged out of her professional demeanor, snatched the papers from Schrubb's hands, and rustled them in Carel's face. "This is serious business."

Carel pulled the phone away from his cheek and spoke in a pedantic tone. "This concerns my daughter. If you'll excuse me."

"We're going to sue you!" The veins popped from Bev's neck. "We're shutting you down! We're taking it all! You might be going to jail! Can't we just get a little bit of your attention?"

Schrubb leaned forward and eased the documents from her hand. "Let's keep ourselves under control."

Bev stepped back and crossed her arms; the blush was still in her cheeks. She spoke directly to Schrubb. "If you had this under control, we wouldn't be here."

Carel stood and moved toward the door while returning to

his call. "Sure. Right now. I'll look for you in the parking lot." He snapped his phone shut and turned to his hosts. "I have something important to take care of. I'll be right back. Don't you go anywhere."

He left Schrubb and Bev staring incredulously at each other.

As soon as he stepped outside, Carel got whacked by the scorching August sun. Sweat beaded on his forehead, while his teeth chattered as if he were shivering. He was caught in a vise between a bank and two marriages—one already failed and the other fixing to. *Where the hell is she?* He put his hands on his knees to catch his breath.

A dinged-up old Ford Super Duty rumbled to the sidewalk in front of him. He raised his head to make out the words *Geische Custom Framing—Construction* ineffectively scraped off the door. Mari shoved the door open for him, and Carel climbed in, thankful for the air-conditioning.

"Hot out there?" Mari piped.

Carel nodded, collecting his breath. "So what's going down here?"

"Like I told you. I need six hundred fifty dollars cash money to get Willow bailed out. You know they're gonna drop the charges like they always do the first time. But I only got some two fifty, and that's all I got." She paused and gave him a moment to do the math in his head. "So if you can spot me four hundred bucks—just four hundred—I'll make Willow pay you back."

"What happened to that Ebberhaus boy? He get locked up too?"

"Traffic violation. They didn't hold him. The stuff was in Willow's purse, and you know her. She wasn't going to lay it on him. So she's the one who got to spend the night in the hoosegow, courtesy of your uncle."

He shifted his body toward her. "You hang on to your two fifty. I'll just go down there and bail her out."

"You?" Mari's laugh was insulting. "She won't come out if it's you."

Carel felt his body stiffen. He rubbed his eyes with his hands. He didn't know that his body was trembling until he felt Mari's calming hand on his shoulder.

"Ca-re-el." She spoke his name like exhaling smoke. "It's not like she's gone and done nothin' we didn't do when we was that age."

"Nothing." Carel pressed back against the car seat as if trying to squeeze himself out of his own skin. "I'm nothing, Mari. I got less than I had when you threw me out. Not a pot to piss in."

She wasn't going to let that pass. "I didn't throw you out, Carel. It was you who went pussy hunting."

He stopped her with the meanest glare he could muster. "That's not entirely true. You goddamn know it."

"It's basically true."

They were locked in a death stare, but neither of them threw any more words. Neither of them wanted to dive back into their failed marriage. That reluctance gave Carel the space to fall back into his current woes.

"I had it right here in my hands, Mari." He clawed up his outstretched hands to show her. "In my hands. Now they got it all. Everything!" He gestured toward the bank with his thumb. "They're taking it all away from me!"

There was a moment of quiet before Mari asked, "This mean you don't have the four hundred?"

"Me! It was going to be me! I was going to be the one Geische who got out from under it all," Carel bawled, thumping his chest. "My daddy couldn't make nothing of himself.

Same goes for Uncle Victor, God rest his soul. Not my *opa* or his father, either. Not one of us made enough so our kids didn't have to start out at the bottom again. Not one of us."

What stopped him was the stunned expression on Mari's face, like she was looking at something she'd never seen before. His eyes were puffy with grief, his teeth clenched in rage. He quickly ran a hand across his eyes, afraid there might be a tear. "But these guys! So high and mighty."

"Ah, you did good for yourself, Carel." Mari was never daunted by his tyranny. "You just got a little too big for your britches. And don't you go feeling sorry for yourself. That was my daddy's land that you sold off to get yourself started. You remember that?"

"A-ach!" Carel let out a screech that sounded like a crow call. He dropped his head against the dashboard. "Oh, goddamn it." Through all the ack-ack flying through his mind, Carel remembered that the deed to Mari's home, the old Hilss farmstead, was wrapped up in that package the bank would be repossessing.

"They're not going to stop with me, Mari. There is no end to what that damn bank will do to us."

"Us?" Mari cocked her head. "Shouldn't you be talking this over with your wife? And not me? I mean, it really ain't my concern that your business went bad."

Carel sulked back against the seat. "Probably gonna lose her, too. This is not what she married me for."

"So what was her secret charm?" A witchy smile crossed Mari's face. "As for me, I just married you 'cause I was pregnant."

"Are you messing with me?" He spoke syllable by syllable, just like he'd say before he slapped her.

They fell again into that cold, hard stare—such a familiar part of their marriage. She played the moment well, letting him simmer as long as she pleased. Then she eased out of it with a joke: "Just sayin' that you've got your own special way with women."

Carel leaned toward her. "Your bitchy little sarcasm is getting me pissed off here."

She grinned into his threat. "What I want is four hundred dollars. You got it or not?"

There was never an easy way out with her. He took a moment to pull himself together before suggesting, "Why don't you just pull into that drive-through line and we'll find out exactly how much I got. Where's my hat?"

"You didn't have no hat when you got in." Mari ground the truck into gear and rolled up to the bank window.

"Hey, Suzi," Carel shouted over her lap to the auto-teller. "Can you tell me what my balance is?"

"Sure thing, Mr. Geische. I can look up your account number, but I have to see your identification."

"It's me! Carel Geische. I went to school with your sister. You know me, Suzi."

"I'm sorry, Mr. Geische, but it's bank policy. I need to see your driver's license or something."

Mari was doing a poor job of stifling her giggle.

"This whole town is going to hell, I tell you." Carel passed his driver's license to Mari, who passed it to the teller.

"When they start calling you Mr. Geische," Mari observed, "that means they're not on your side anymore."

There was $708.62 in the account. Carel took $700 in cash, counted out $400 for Mari and folded the rest into his shirt pocket.

"I'll be needing this," he told Mari as he got out of the truck.

Bev was no longer in the bank manager's office when Carel returned. Schrubb was slouched over his computer.

"God, are you guys brave." Carel snatched his Resistol off of Schrubb's desk.

Schrubb looked up at his old friend. "What?"

"You didn't have to call me in. You could have just done all this by certified mail."

Schrubb sat up and addressed him frankly. "We're going to have to break the news to Mari. I just wanted to give you the chance to talk to her first."

Carel stuffed his hat on his head. "I just talked to her."

The two men parted without shaking hands.

• • •

Max found he was an odd visitor in his parents' home. He stayed in his nephews' bedroom through the weekend and into the following week. He saw his father's antics as just that: antics designed to keep everyone focused on him. Still, Max got a kick out of his time with the kids, throwing footballs in the backyard and keeping them up late at night with quiet board games played in the heat of the upstairs bedroom.

Judging by the family photos that cluttered the mantels and hallways, Max had died after high school. The most recent photo hung at the dark end of a hall. It was his senior picture, mounted and framed, with a verse that his mother had created in needlepoint.

For this son of mine was dead and is alive again;
He was lost and is found. So they began to celebrate.
LUKE 15:24, The Prodigal Son

In reality, this was the work of his father, who undoubtedly manipulated his mother's hand—the subtle and cruel means that his father used to twist his mother's impression of her oldest son. He hated the old man for that.

At Jock's insistence, Max brought his smashed-up muscle car into Ritzi Agricultural Equipment for repair.

"I didn't know you did body work. I thought all you did was fix broken sickles on hay swathers." Max laid a cagey glance on his brother. "Does *opa* know about this?"

"Kinda. Just don't go talking it up around him." Jock displayed more humor and confidence in his shop than he had with his father. "A man can make more money around here fixing toilets in RVs than he can repairing harvesters and windrowers." It was Jock's turn to give Max the wily look. "Do you want flames?"

"What?"

"Flames. My guys can airbrush some neat-looking flames on your fender. Done it to a few cars, you know." Then, lowering his voice and smiling through his secret: "*Opa* don't know about that, neither."

The old shop seemed much larger than Max remembered it, or maybe it was less cluttered. The value of the property itself afforded Jock good bank credit. His little brother had grown up to be one of the clean-shirt, cowboy-hatted businessmen of the town rather than the dirt-under-the-fingernails working man their father had been.

Jock led his brother into his air-conditioned office, where the Hunters Extravaganza brochures and plans for a show booth lay out among all the other stuff strewn across their father's old desk.

Max picked up a brochure. "So, are you going to do those hunters' shows?"

Jock plopped into the chair behind his desk without removing his Resistol. "Na. I'm going to wait to see what *opa* says."

"Why the hell are you going to do that?" Max was left standing, not sure what to do with the boxes and piles of papers and debris that occupied the chairs on his side of the desk. "It's you who has to make the payroll around here. Papa don't know what's going on anymore, and you have the right idea."

"It's just that . . ." Jock cast his eyes aside. "That's just it, Max. I don't know if I'm right."

That comment showed Max how thoroughly the old man controlled the very thought process of his youngest son. "You just hang on, Jock. He's going to pop off pretty soon, and then you can make this place work the way that it should."

"Don't you be so damn cold, Max," Jock snapped back. "He's had a hard life. You saw how sick he is."

"He chose the hard life, Jock. It didn't have to be so hard. Not for him. Not for Mama. Not for Gerdie, you, or me."

"Oh, that's great advice coming from you, big brother. You just run off down the highway when things get tough." Jock rummaged through some papers on his desk, as if he might find his next words there. "Talk about hurting people. Nothing ever hurt Mama more than you running out on us."

"Ran out? No damn way, little brother. I was run out of this town. Not by vigilantes, I remind you. Not by the deacons of Zion Lutheran Church, but by your poor, sickly father. One hard-life man cut my future for me, and he's doing it to you too, Jock!"

Jock sat up to protest, but Max cut him short.

"Why do you think you don't have the balls to run your own shop?" Max snatched up a brochure off the desk and threw it against Jock's chest.

Jock shooed the paper away and backed away, his mouth sealed.

Max felt terrible—it was just the way his old man would have acted. Still finding no place to sit, he toned down a bit. "You know, Jock, chasing me out was the greatest gift the old man ever gave me. It set me out of his shadow and let me be myself. And that is something that you will never get from him."

Earlier they had talked about going to lunch when Max brought in his car, but the mood had soured. Jock clenched his jaws, said he had some business to attend to, and suggested they make it up sometime later that week.

Max figured it was best to just walk it off, and he set off through the pecan shade along old San Antonio Street. He turned up to Main Street to check out all the fancy boutiques that were replacing the old hardware stores and garages he'd grown up with. Passing through his childhood playground, now the town's Marktplatz, he crossed over to the Altdorf Biergarten, where he arrived in a light sweat.

The outdoor beer garden fell in the shadow of the St. Mary's bell tower. Beer barrel tables stood under red-and-white umbrellas stamped with the logos of old-world brews. To clinch the old-world ambiance and attract tourists, the waitresses wore dirndls—those tight, boob-lifting, waist-cinching dresses that Bavarian women wore at their festivals.

Max strolled casually along the garden's picket fence, eyeing the waitresses who suffered through the merciless midday Texas sun, before he slipped through the low gate to choose his seat. His server came to him looking much like the classic St. Pauli Girl, with the exception of the speck of jewelry in her nose. She stood before him and launched into her waitress spiel, explaining the differences between the biers: Weiss, Hefeweizen, and Spaten Optimator. "That last one will put you on your ass on a hot day like this."

"Well, then I'll have the Optimator."

"That all?"

"No. I'll have the house salad, too."

That took her by surprise. "Really?"

"Yep." He nodded.

"The salad bowl is only about this size." She demonstrated the size with her cupped hands. There was a Band-Aid around her ring finger, where Max guessed that she may have burned herself in the kitchen.

He smiled and nodded to confirm his order.

"House salad and Optimator," she repeated, to be sure they were both clear about the order.

"Yes." Max made a broad gesture with his hands. "*Ein großes Optimator.*"

That roused a laugh from her, and she took a moment to look him up and down. "So you're from around here?"

"You disappointed?"

"I usually save that beer spiel for the tourists." She snapped the menu from him as she turned to leave. "They drop better tips."

He kept an eye on her after he was served, almost—but not quite—ogling her. In spite of the dirndl, she came off as a thoroughly modern kind of girl; no makeup, that little jewel thing in her nose, and that subtly sarcastic manner. When he was down to the bottom of his *Optimator,* she sat at his table while totaling the tab. She gave him a cocky eye and held the tab just out of his reach.

"So, how do we know each other?"

"You're Willow Geische." He didn't reach out for the tab. "I'm Max Ritzi."

"Oh? Oh! You're Jock's big brother. Maximilian and Evelyn's son."

He nodded.

"Then we're kin on my dad's side. Or something like that."

It charmed him to see her get excited about that. "Yeah. Carel and I are first cousins."

"Yeah. You're the one who ran away. California or Canada or something, right?"

"Well, I was in California at one time, but I'm coming home from Arizona now. Flagstaff."

"Coming home."

"Well, it's fair weekend and all."

"Yeah. Mom's been talking about that. You'll see her there." She was staring at him, maybe trying to remember him. "So what happened to your head?"

"Bumped into a steering wheel."

"Oh." She seemed oddly offended.

To keep her there for another moment, Max quickly turned the conversation to her. "And what are you doing with yourself?"

She shrugged her shoulders playfully. "Workin' here."

"For the summer?"

"Since I finished school."

"When was that? This spring?"

"Spring before last. Graduated a year early. Wanted to get out."

"And you've been working here all that time?"

"Yeah, kinda regular now. I know. Didn't get out too far, did I?"

"I didn't mean anything rude. I'm sorry."

"It's okay. Just working here. Won't be here much longer."

"Oh?" Max smiled, hopeful that she had a plan to get out of town. "What are you doing?"

"Gettin' married."

Instinctively he glanced at her ring finger. "So the ring didn't fit?" he tried to make a joke.

It wasn't funny to her. "Somethin' like that." She took out a cloth and started wiping the table. "It's what ya do 'round here."

"Is he a local man, or are you running off to someplace new?"

"High school sweethearts, ya know. It's kinda expected."

"Oh sure. I know all about that." Max gave a half laugh and noticed how intently she focused on his every word. Her smile was warm, genuine, and naïve, too.

"He's a good guy. Ain't got nothin'. We'll be moving onto my mom's place. Good worker, and we'll make something of it. Get it going the way my *opa* had it running. It'll be our little happily-ever-after."

"That's nice." Max risked another probe. "And how is your mom doing?"

"Fine."

There was a long moment when Max thought she might be figuring him out. Then Willow just said she had to get back to "workin' here," and they casually agreed to see each other around.

"To explore our genealogy," Willow remarked.

"That could be treacherous stuff." He left her a noticeably large tip. Something more than a tourist would have left.

• • •

Stuck in the slow days of mid-August, Max found it hard to get his business going. His family, still living in the forgotten past of this antique town, had no need for the Internet, so he had to use the rudimentary connections provided for tourists in the new coffeehouses and at the public library. Then he would go out and grab a beer with Heinie, Rickie, and Buddy, and they would sit in the grandstand watching the varsity football practices. No one on the coaching staff much remembered Max, but he made an effort to corner a coach here and there so he could pitch the Power Patch, without much success.

The best time to catch up with Willow, Max figured, was well after the lunch hour, when the table umbrellas had lost their ability to protect the tourist from the afternoon sun.

Willow was flirtatious. "Is this an *Optimator* afternoon?" She brought his beer before he asked and, once again, sat talking with him as she tallied up his check. They got talking about cars, and Max bragged on the pitch-black Challenger that was now in his brother's garage.

"So you're without wheels too?"

"No. Jock is my *Kleiner Verdruß*," Max responded, using the old German idiom for "small annoyance" in place of *Bruder*. "I made him lend me his truck until he gets mine fixed."

"Family cars. Tell me about it," she started. "I lent my truck to my *Mutter Verdruß* the other night." They laughed at her play on his words. "No, it was a few nights back. Now she's workin', and I gotta get out to Luckenbach and find it."

She ripped the check from her pad and laid it on the table before him with an expression that Max found hard to interpret. She had her jaw set like she was spoiling for a fight, but there was an inviting twinkle in her eye.

"Either got lucky or got busted, I guess." She smiled at the stunned reaction that got from him. "It's okay. My mother has lots of friends. She made it home in one piece."

Max nodded, encouraging her on.

"But my truck is still out there." She let out a big sigh, and in one fluid movement stood up in that long skirt they made her wear and started to turn away.

"I can give you a ride," Max called out to stop her. "I'm already off for the day."

Willow stopped and seemed to think about that for a minute, then smiled broadly to him. "That'd be cool."

The two of them driving off together, Max knew, left lots of fodder for small-town gossip—everyone in town would know.

On the drive out to Luckenbach, Max tried to start up a conversation about her life with her mother and asked how that was going to change when she got married.

"I don't know." Willow turned the question back on him. "Now, how do you fit in? My dad's cousin, right?"

"Yeah. My mama is your *oma's* half-sister. Your dad and I were kids together. Your mother too. Saw a lot of each other because our parents were tight."

"Then . . . ?" She turned in her seat to pull more out of him with her silent stare.

"Then your folks got married, and I got out of town." This line of conversation was starting to make Max feel uncomfortable.

She was brazen. "You were the one who got jilted, then?"

"Yeah. You might say that."

"So, you still hot for my mom?" she teased. "That what brought ya back?"

"Shit, no. We were your age then."

"I'm getting married." She sat forward. "Think I'm doing the right thing?"

There was a sudden dip in the road and a low water crossing that had Max focus on his driving as they splashed their way to the other side of the creek.

"Do you love him?"

Again she turned the conversation back to him. "Did you love her?"

"Who? Your mom?" That took him completely by surprise, and he took his eyes off the road to look at her. It was a trick question, like she was luring him into admitting that love doesn't last or hold a marriage together. He faked a laugh. "Nah. We just grew up together."

Luckenbach hadn't changed at all since he'd been there last. There was the same old clapboard dance hall across from the made-to-look-dilapidated general store/post office/beer joint all in one rambling henhouse of a building. Loitering about the porch on that weekday afternoon sat a brood of guitar-pickers who rearranged the lyrics of made-over Waylon Jennings songs while Winnebago-loads of visitors walked around snapping pictures of the honky-tonk and buying souvenir T-shirts.

Gone were the rows of cars that had made a parking lot out of the back pasture for Saturday night's dance. There was no guessing at which truck was Willow's—it stood out there as lonely as the last cow in the corral, an oversized black Ford Super Duty Dually with a *Piss On Chevy* window sticker. An old company logo had been crudely sanded off the door, but Max could still see the faint outline of a star and part of the words that had once been *Geische Custom Framing—Construction.*

"My dad gave it to me, so I just have to pay for gas and insurance," Willow explained as she pulled the door open. A beer bottle rolled onto the ground. She looked at it, then gathered up her skirts, climbed in, and cranked and cajoled the engine to start. After a bit of fussing, the truck fired up with a roar that would scare off any college boy who tried to crawl in there with her.

"He really meant it for my mom," Willow shouted from the driver's seat. "Just because he's got an attitude and can't bring himself to give her anything, even though he owns half the friggin' buildings in this town." She left the engine running and jumped to the ground. "Works for her, though. She really doesn't want anything from him."

Max was leaning against the fender. "Well, girl, he doesn't own Luckenbach. And he doesn't own you."

Her smile pleased him, like he'd said something right. She stepped up to Max with that flirtatious smile. "You gonna buy me a beer, mister?"

"You old enough?"

"I think you are." She smiled in that way that promised boys more than she intended.

• • •

"Hey, Road Trip. Heard you were back." Slaps on the back and high fives.

"Max? That really you?" Smiles and handshakes.

"Good to see you again, man. How was it up in Utah?"

"Welcome home, dude. Get ya a beer?"

"Sure. I'll take a beer." This was more like the welcome home that Max had imagined. "And I've never been to Utah."

"Really? We heard you had seven wives up there." Laughs all around.

Max was walking into the fairgrounds with his old gang: Aubrey and Addy along with the gridiron brothers—Heinie Ortner, Rickie Boensch, and Buddy Nuweinkraus. He wasn't riding into glory in his muscle car like he had planned, but he was sliding right into the cozy surety of his past.

"I was out there, man." He swept his arms in a large semi-circle over his head. "I was out there."

The fair hadn't even started. The carnival rides were still being rigged. Yet the stock-show crowd had come for the free beer and cabrito laid out by the Texas Sheep & Goat Breeders

Association—loudest party in town and not an *auslander* among them. Lots of tight-ass blue jeans and big, shady cowboy hats.

"Hey, Road Trip, ya wanna buy some property? Now that you're back in town."

"Yeah, Heinie's gone into the real estate business, ya know."

When they all laughed, Max grinned along with them. He couldn't see Heinie as a real estate man.

"Go ahead and tell 'em, Heinie. Max is one of those money-bags comin' in from California. Buyin' up the town."

"I'm not coming in from California . . ."

"Yeah, my dad's place burned down." Heinie's head bobbed up and down, keeping time with his words. "I'm gonna sell it."

"I'm sorry to hear that." Max's brow crinkled with sincerity. "Did you get insurance money? Can't you rebuild?"

That comment raised an odd round of laughter from the gang, but Heinie wasn't laughing. "Naw. Think I can get more selling the lot to some money-bag from out of town. Easier than wrestling with the insurance company."

Max was smiling along with the joke that he didn't understand as he scanned the crowd, and there was Carel, standing at the far end of the lot like he just stepped off the cover of a country music CD. Carel's gun-sight gaze locked in on Max. There was an unusual gap in the sea of partiers, a sort of open gangway between the cousins. The silence that stretched between them was heavier than all the party chatter, the guffaws of his own gang, and the band tuning up on a short platform down by the racetrack.

In that frozen moment Mari stepped out of the crowd and into the corridor that lay between the two men. Her first glance was toward Carel. She must have caught the intensity of her ex-husband's hard stare, because she turned slowly to follow its direction, her sundress fluttering about her knees as her fingers raked the wild hair across her forehead.

Max watched the smile fall from her face. It was the first time they'd laid eyes on each other since he'd left Texas in Aubrey's busted-up Camaro, nearly twenty years back. She had kept her slight, boyish features but looked a bit worn-out—in the sun a lot, he guessed. It seemed she'd never figured out what to do with that stringy black hair of hers. Max held back to see if she would come to him for a sociable greeting or even a quick embrace, but instead she shot a quick glance back at Carel before stepping back into the anonymity of the crowd like a jackrabbit ducking for cover behind a stump—leaving only Carel's focused glare.

Max cracked a subtly arrogant snicker and took a deliberately long, slow draw from his beer without breaking eye contact. Their lock on each other was disrupted by an old friend's voice.

"Hey, Road Trip. What's goin' on with you?"

Max switched into his salesman persona. "Hey, Milt. Heard you're the big JV coach now."

"How true it is, Max. Got all the little ones going up the line."

"That's great, because I've got something that can really help their performance. Have you ever heard of the Power Patch?" Max went to work as they drifted off to get another beer.

Over his shoulder, Max caught Carel, still there at the far end of the yard, spoiling for the fight that didn't happen.

After fetching a drink and running off the JV coach with his sales pitch, Max was left alone with his beer. He spotted Brady Casbier, off in the shade of the racetrack grandstands. The oversized newspaper man had a large camera dangling from his neck and seemed to be interviewing someone. Welcome or not, Max strode the distance between them and jumped into their conversation.

The interviewee was Thea, who seemed grateful for his interruption. She looked Max up and down before declaring, "My, my. I can see the years have been good to you, Mr. Ritzi."

"Why, thank you. I think." Max nodded, basking in her favor. "You did mean that as a compliment, didn't you?"

That comment got a twinkle from Thea but a cold, non-verbal response from Brady. Thea's attempts to chat with Max seemed stifled by Brady's rolling eyes and caused her to scoot off with some frail excuse. Brady kept his humorless eyes on her as she walked away.

"Did I break up something here?"

"No. Not really." Brady turned to Max, the camera swinging across his chest like some obtuse amulet. He was such a geek. "What are you up to?"

"Well, Brady, I'm bringing a business to town. Hear you're the man to talk to about some advertising."

"What kind of business? But first, let me tell you: It's not like it was when you left. You're going to have a hard time getting a storefront in this town. Even if you are lucky enough to find something . . . Rents are through the roof."

"Don't need it. I'm doing a network marketing business."

Brady screwed up his eyes like a dog watching TV. "I'm not sure I know what that is." When Max started in on his explanation, Brady held up his hand. "Great. I want to hear all about it, but let's get together when we're not drunk."

"Drunk?"

Only then did Brady laugh. And at what? Max found him just plain weird.

They started drifting together with short, purposeless steps, away from the party crowds, as Brady caught Max up on old high school friends: who had moved off, who had passed away, who was still married, who was getting divorced, who was available.

Max had to ask. "Mari still on her dad's land?"

"She sure is. My kids spend a lot of time over there."

"Really?"

"Willow watches them for me. She's like their big sister, so we're kind of like family." When Brady came to a stop, his camera banged against his chest. His eyes narrowed. "You're not back here to mess with things, are you?"

"What do you mean by that?" Max asked, with more of a challenge in his voice than he'd intended.

"You come back after Mari, or what?" The two men took a moment to study each other, divining each other's intentions. Brady's words could have been a warning. "Mari's doing all right. They both are."

"Dang it, Brady." Max slapped his shoulder. "I didn't come home to relive my high school days. That was way back when. I came back to get my business going."

Brady's demeanor changed. He slapped Max on the shoulder while holding his camera against his chest. "You come see me about that advertising. I'd like to hear more about that new business of yours."

Max looked around and tried to figure out how they had come to be so far away from the crowd. The lights of the casita over the beer and cabrito grew brighter as the sun faded from the sky. The band, up against the racetrack, had started up, and the crowd tightened in front of their little stage. The dancing was under way.

"I'm off to the midway, Max. I'm doing an exposé on how the parents of Fredericksburg are going to put their children on rides that were put together by transient druggies and paroled pedophiles."

Max stopped. "Are they really?"

In that weird Brady way of scrunching up his face, he gave his answer with the inflection of a question. "That's what I'm going to find out?"

Max turned back to the party crowd, where the first people he came upon were gathered around his sister and Jeanie . . . *What last name was she using now?* They were pouring home-made margaritas out of a thermos, which was making them quite popular at the moment.

Droopy-eyed and limbered with margarita, Jeanie stepped into him. "Heard you were back, Mr. Road Trip." She slid her arms around his neck, careful not to spill her drink. It was an uncomfortably sensuous embrace for Max, especially with his sister so close at hand. Jeanie's tequila breath was so strong that he got a rush like he'd just thrown back a shot himself. Her knee was pressing its way up the inside of his thigh, toward his crotch. He turned a cheek to the kiss she was fixing to plant on his lips.

Instead of kissing him, though, she whispered in a slurred, seductive tone, "My brother wanted me to find out how long you were going to be in town for."

"And just how were you going to get that information?" he responded in a conversational voice. "You going to take me into your bedroom and interrogate me?"

Gerdie heard that part and stepped forward. "Get away from her, Max." She actually pushed against him. "This is your cousin you're coming on to. And"—her eyes widened as she suddenly recalled—"you're a married man!"

"Am I?" He untangled himself from Jeanie.

"Are you?" Gerdie had been swilling margaritas and wasn't in a condition to figure things out too quickly. "Oh, Max, did you screw up another one? Is that why you came back?"

Oh, the rumors that would start if he said nothing . . . He

just teased his sister with a sarcastic grin and turned away to leave her guessing.

The thicket of partiers had fallen into shadows and silhouettes. Max elbowed his way through them in search of his clique. It was darker now, and fewer people stepped up to greet him than when he had arrived. The next familiar face he stumbled past was Thea in her little black dress and cowboy boots.

Thea spoke first. "You lose your dance partner, mister?"

"Yeah. I did." He cocked his head toward the dance floor. "You want to give it a go?"

Thea took a long last drink from her beer, and they dropped their bottles simultaneously into a nearby trash barrel. Max took that as a yes.

He snatched her hand and stepped into the swirls and eddies of dancing couples scuffing about to a rocked-up, rehashed old Merle Haggard song. Round and round, guys with eyes hid under the brims of cowboy hats pushed willing girls backwards in the quick-quick, slow-slow pace of a Texas two-step.

The warm night breeze, the dizzy turns of the dance, the buzz of all those afternoon beers, and the feel of a woman pressed up against him—this was the bed of roses that Max had come home to find. Thea was prancing surely under his lead, but her eyes ran around the dance floor as if she had accepted his dance on a bet. To win a second go-round—and Max wanted that—he backed away from those luscious boobs of hers and allowed some air between them. Now they could see each other's eyes and flow together in that quick-quick, slow-slow, all smiles and fun.

They danced to a second song, then a third, and maybe a fourth before they headed off the floor with sweat rolling down their backs.

"You made a mess out of me, Mr. Max Ritzi." Thea latched

onto Max's arm as they wove their way to the sidelines. "Don't look at me. I am a mess." She fanned herself with her hand.

"Ah, but what a lovely mess you are," Max cracked back to her.

"Is my face all red? I feel flushed."

"You look happy to me."

Crossing under a string of sixty-watt bulbs at the far end of the casita, Max caught a glimpse of the bobbling black hat of his pal Heinie Ortner. He pulled Thea off in that direction.

"Let me get you a beer."

"Sure." Thea smiled but pulled away. "But let's say hi to Carel first."

They had nearly stumbled into Carel, who was sitting at a picnic table with his back to them. The seats alongside him were occupied by guys in cowboy hats, each with a stack of red plastic beer cups piled up in front of him. Heinie, with his black hat, crawled into a space directly across from Carel.

"I'll be over here by the bar." Max bowed out as Thea slipped away toward the popular table. Carel twisted in his seat to greet her.

Then Heinie's voice boomed across the table, loud enough for Max to hear. "So, Carel. Miss Beverly said she seen you down at the bank this afternoon. Ya get any of that letter of intent money? Ya know, for that little deal we got?"

Carel leaned across the table, causing Heinie to ease back a little bit. Not that he was intentionally eavesdropping, but Max could hear the ominous tone in Carel's voice. "You want to know what happened to me at that bank, buddy? I'll tell you what those scumbags . . ."

Carel's wife, sitting to his left, arched in to mute him. Max couldn't hear what she said, but Carel's response was meant for all: "They're not from here. They don't give a shit about us." He was shouting now. "Those grubby shysters shut me down. When it's all said and done"—he pointed across the table—"Heinie had the right idea! Those sons of bitches."

Carel's wife was tugging on his sleeve.

"Oh sure, they think they can buy us all!" Carel came out of his seat like he was ready to fight. "Well, I say come and take it."

A cagey little grin crept across Max's face, a passive salute to Carel's demise.

Thea turned and walked away from what was taking the shape of a volatile situation.

"Come and take it!" Carel punched at the air—his wife trying to calm him, others egging him on. "Those *auslanders* have not seen the last of Carel Geische!"

Thea shook her head as she returned to Max. "I hate to see him like this."

"That is the only way I remember him," Max replied as they turned to collect their drinks. "Back when we were kids running together, that blustering of his got me out of trouble on more than one occasion."

"You?" Thea bade him continue.

"Yeah. My cousin. He even took a serious whupping for me one time." Max chuckled at the memory as they turned to keep an eye on the Carel show.

Carel was on the stump now. "They're stealing our town right out from under us. I tell you, Heinie, they're going to get it all." He had an audience beyond his table cheering him on. "Our streets are going to be nothing but a string of strip malls. Gonna look like Kerrville. Just a bunch of ugly old chain stores owned by bankers in Houston."

As Max and Thea drifted away, they could hear the whistles and cheers from anonymous voices out of the dark, goading

Carel. The row of big hats at the picnic table dipped up and down. *You tell 'em, Carel.*

Thea turned her attention back to Max: "A whupping? Huh."

"Yeah. We were kids. Typical Texas kids. This one time, we got caught." Max was thinking he should stop there, but Thea's eyes pried for more, spoiling for him to take it further.

"It was back at his uncle Victor's place. Messing with the man's worthless, old, worn-out rodeo horses. Mari was in on it too. Back then she was always running with me and Carel."

"And . . . ?" Thea lay her hand on his chest, light as a butterfly.

"We were trying to hide in the barn. Both my old man and that drunken uncle of Carel's coming after us—one with a mesquite switch, the other taking off his belt." Max glanced back over at his cousin, still full of spit and vinegar. "Yeah. We'd been had."

"So. What happened to you?"

"Me? I was hiding up by the door, sure to be the first one caught. But no. When they come in, Carel just jumped out of the loft. They grabbed hold of him, dragged him outside, bent him over the old picnic table out by that cooker, and whaled on his ass for us all to hear."

"That's terrible." Thea pulled her hand away.

"That's Carel."

Their attention returned to the table, where it sounded like Carel was making a campaign promise. "I'm not taking it. You shouldn't take it either. We're a lot more Texan than that, aren't we?" He had the mob all riled up, whooping and shouting. "They are not going to buy up the history of Gillespie County and sell it off to a mob of sissy-ass tourists!"

His wife managed to pull him back down to his seat.

Someone brought him a fresh beer. With Carel back in his seat, they could hear the band once again.

"Carel was a big help to me when I was getting my business started here," Thea told Max. "I found him to be a generous guy. As a kid, when I dropped out of 4-H . . ." She trailed off. "You know how all the others start to shun you?"

"Yeah." Max nodded. "I know whatcha mean."

"Well, Carel didn't do that. He stayed friends with me."

"Yeah. He can be like that, too."

There was more that happened in that barn than Max was willing to tell. He didn't say how Mari had crept up to the door where he hid when Carel was taking the licking for the three of them, how they grabbed onto one another while listening to Carel's wails and cries. They were scared together, just teens, and Mari kissed him—wet and deep. It was the first taste of raw lust Max had ever known, and it stood him up with a fear and fervor that hadn't been resolved to this day.

The phone in Thea's pocket buzzed. The friends she'd come with were fixing to leave, so they parted with a neighborly hug and some quick words. "I'm going to be tied down at the store all weekend. I'm hoping it's going to be really busy in town. With those sissy-ass tourists and all."

"I'm going to be at my parents' house. Hope it won't be busy there." He didn't feel right asking her out. Officially he was still married. "I'm not going to be doing any shopping."

"The Cody Dodger Band is at the fair Saturday night." She started to turn away. "Save me a dance, okay?"

He watched her walk off to find her friends.

"Nice juicy ass, there." Buddy Nuweinkraus had come creeping up behind him. "You ever wonder what she's got going on under that dress? I mean, she's got that panty store and all."

Max looked at the melted cheeks of his old pal. Buddy smelled like a distillery on a pot farm. "Yeah. I've been wondering about that all night."

"Come on. We're hanging out down by the starting gates. Rickie's got the hooch."

• • •

Rickie always had the hooch—a clear moonshine passed around in a mason jar. To the cheers of his drinking buddies, he twisted off the lid and tossed it over his shoulder so they would be committed to finishing off the home-stilled poison before they called it a night—a bonding ritual since high school. But this was some twenty years on. Max figured it was amusing for schoolkids but a pretty sick habit for grown-ups with school-children of their own at home. Yet when the jar was passed to him, he took a swig.

"To savage nights of shame and puke." Buddy held the jar overhead.

"Cowards would avoid this, but we are . . . ," shouted Rickie, suddenly forgetting his words.

"We are made of the sterner stuff!" someone else said, completing the inane toast.

In a fog of his own, Max saw the ghosts of his old pals, the best of his friends, clinging hard to their traditions. Out there at the fairgrounds, under the tracers of an August meteor shower, the tribe was chanting, "They are weak but we are strong! They are weak but we are strong!" when a pair of Gillespie County sheriff's cruisers pulled up and one uniformed officer stepped out of each car.

"*Wie gehts*, Lester. You finally get off work?" Heinie sassed at them.

"Or them sheep down in the show barn been complainin' we're keepin' them up?" another man cracked.

"Hey," Buddy chimed in. "We got some cold beer here for you."

"*Geht nich*, boys. I'm still on duty." Deputy Lester Metzger took it in with a professional humor. "But if any of you boys get behind the wheel of your vehicle, we'll be waiting for you with a breathalyzer."

While Lester chatted amicably with his former classmates, Max noticed that his partner took up a position behind them. They were here on business.

Lester had graduated high school with them—he'd been with the football squad as team manager. Back then he was a squirrelly guy who brought towels to the real players. Although still smaller in size than any of them, he towered over them with authority as he asked the group, "Have any of you fine, upstanding citizens seen Miss Willow Geische out here tonight?"

"Little Willow? Carel's kid?"

Lester rolled his cop-like glance toward Max, who was suddenly figuring out that this was about him. In that moment he pulled himself into a state of complete sobriety.

"Naw. She wasn't out here," Buddy answered.

"We're not her crowd. We're a bunch of whisky-drinkin' old farts," Heinie quipped, getting a laugh from the gang.

"You might find her back in town with them wine drinkers," Rickie called out from the back of the crowd.

"Drinkin' white wine and listening to jazz music." All the hooch drinkers seemed to think that was funny.

Lester smiled at their inebriated wisecracks, but it was an official-looking smile. "Well, her father asked us to check. Seems that she didn't make it home tonight."

"Lucky gal," someone catcalled, begetting another round of laughter as well as a follow-up gibe: "We'd be so lucky."

Max kept quiet, suspicious about the presence of the county sheriff's office and uncomfortable with his friends' comments about Willow.

"If any of you gentlemen happen to see her, would you please let me know? Just so we can tell Mr. Geische that we did our job."

"Which Mr. Geische? Carel or the sheriff?" That was another one they found funny.

"Both." Lester's terse answer put an end to the laughter.

While the other officer, the one Max didn't know, started up a conversation with Heinie, Rickie, and Buddy, Lester stepped over to Max. "I need a word with you, Max."

"Sure." He saw then that drawing the others off was some kind of cop trick to save Max the embarrassment of being singled out.

"Over by my car." Lester waited until his partner joined them back at the cruiser before he told Max, "The sheriff wants to talk with you."

"Yeah? Why don't I just come around and visit him during office hours?"

"That's just not his way, Max." Lester looked at him in a way that let Max know that this was going to happen. "The last anyone saw of Miss Geische, you were procuring alcohol for her out at Luckenbach."

"That's bullshit, Lester. You can't just—"

"Procuring alcohol for a minor is a still a crime in Gillespie County." Lester's words stopped Max's back talk. "And the sheriff said he needs to clear up some questions he has about an old restraining order with your name on it."

"That fucking restraining order has expired—"

"You can come along as my guest or I can arrest you, Max."

"This is Carel, isn't it, Lester? That sniveling . . ." Max could feel the blood surging up his neck. "I can't believe this shit!"

Lester slowly pulled a card out of his breast pocket and began to read from it. "You have the right to remain silent . . ."

"Damn it, Lester . . ."

Lester's partner stepped quietly up to Max, almost touching but not quite. He placed his hand on the set of handcuffs kept in a small leather case attached to his belt.

"You can stop reading that shit, Lester." Max stepped to the cruiser and opened the back door himself.

• • •

At the Law Enforcement Center, Max was told once again that he was not yet under arrest. He was asked to wait until the sheriff arrived, and told, "He's usually here first thing in the morning."

Max spent what was left of the night in an uncomfortable plastic chair in the office break room, fuming that Carel had the gall and the wherewithal to pull this off. He was sticky in the shirt he'd been wearing for so long, uncomfortable trying to rest his head on the table, and fading in and out of sleep until roused by the night jailer, who put his hand on Max's shoulder and said, "Come on, now. Sheriff's here."

When Max crossed through the sterile foyer of the Law Enforcement Building, he saw his mother, dressed for church, sitting on a wooden bench and chatting amicably with her brother-in-law, Sheriff Otto Geische. They were talking about the old 4-H. Before he became sheriff, Otto had been a stock-show judge when Evelyn was active in 4-H, and now the two of them were going on about this one and that one and how proud they were of those youngsters out there today at the fair with their sheep and goats.

"While everything else up here is changing so fast . . . ," Otto was saying as Max approached them, unshaven and tired.

"Oh, my dear," Evelyn said as the sheriff turned his head to see his first appointment of the day.

"Come on, Otto. Leave my mother out of this." Then, directly to his mother: "I'm not under arrest, Mama. We're just clearing up some misunderstandings."

"Yes, son, we need to talk." Otto's reply carried a sheriff-like tone of official courtesy. Then, turning back to his sister-in-law with a smile: "This will only take a couple of minutes, Evelyn. I won't make you late for church."

Max followed the sheriff into his office and slammed the door deliberately behind them. Otto lowered himself into his chair on the far side of the desk. Then he let Max blow.

"I could sue your goddamn ass for this." Max, still standing, put his fists on the sheriff's desk and leaned in. "And about that court order shit, way back when, that was all a bunch of bullshit your nephew put down. It was all a lie to run me off. And you goddamn know it."

"It's Sunday, Max. Mind your language."

"You should have checked that out before you sent Lester out to embarrass me in front of my friends."

The sheriff nodded, his dispassion egging Max on.

"If you hadn't been so lazy, you would have checked it out and stopped it!"

Otto waited for a pause in Max's diatribe and spoke slowly. "No. I wouldn't." He made room for a thought. "See, Max, I'm just a simple lawman. It is in my blood to go busting down doors and kicking some ass."

Otto's cool detachment had something of a calming effect on Max.

"My problem is, *kleiner* Max, that I have been such an effective cop here for so long, I don't often get to take advantage of the rare opportunities you present when you come back into town just asking for me to get into your business." Otto pointed a hard finger at Max, then gestured for him to take a seat in the chair across the desk from him.

Max obliged.

With Max seated, Otto leaned back and spoke in a calm, matter-of-fact tone. "My blood nephew, your cousin—an upstanding, contributing citizen of this town—thinks you are some kind of pervert." He let the words settle on Max. "A danger to his kid."

Max shot forward in his seat. "Well, he—"

Otto held up his bear claw to quiet him. "Your turn to listen." Max leaned back and let the sheriff continue. "Some time ago you earned yourself something of a reputation stalking Carel's wife."

"There was no wife. They weren't married."

Otto ignored him. "Now he has reason to believe that you've come back stalking after his daughter." Max lurched forward to respond, but the sheriff blasted back at him. "And your behavior seems to be bearing out his view of things."

"I gave her a ride to pick up her mother's truck."

"That is what I am talking about. It is that kind of behavior that makes you what we, in law enforcement, call a person of suspicion."

Otto's words rolled over Max. "You know what's going on here, Otto. It's Carel. I am not doing anything—"

"Don't you concern yourself with him, *kleiner* Max," the sheriff said. "Your cousin Carel has filed a complaint, and I am desperately looking to find grounds for action on my part. No, I haven't found it. Yet." Up came the bear claw again. "But I want to warn you, Max Ritzi, that we are going to be all over you."

Max didn't flinch.

"You had your little visit. You got drunk with your buddies, and my guess is that you're planning to leave town right after the county fair."

There was a long, dry poker stare between them.

"I'm not going anywhere, Otto."

"You're not planning to stay too long, are you?"

Max paused to allow the tension to abate. "My father is finally fading out. I need to be here for my mama when he's gone. Both my sister and my little brother are . . . well, they're not doing well with all this. And I have already had my full share of small-town bullies pushing me around. You're just another one of them, Otto."

"That's Sheriff Otto to you, son."

Max shook his head at that. "Well, Sheriff, I'm telling you I'm back home now."

Otto stared at him for a while. "Here's your warning." He held up that big hand of his and counted out on his fat fingers so that Max could make a list in his head.

Index finger: "You avoid your cousin Carel. Don't cross tracks with him." Middle finger: "And don't be upsetting his ex-wife either. If you get either one of them pissed off, then you'll be in trouble with me." Then, raising his voice on his ring finger: "And you stay away from that girl too."

Max held up his little finger. "Nothing on the pinkie, Sheriff?"

Otto's mouth grew tight. "You don't let this come to any kind of disturbance. You back off when he comes at you. No fists, no weapons, no ugly words. You don't even respond to him when he unleashes his foul mouth on you."

Max saw the setup: Carel had the law on his side. Inwardly, Max was seething, but he kept his cool, sarcastic demeanor to show Otto he would not be intimidated.

"As long as you are in Gillespie County, I can choose to make your life miserable."

"I learned that in high school, Otto. It's nice to see how some things around here never changed at all." Without waiting to be excused, he stood up and left the office, slamming the door behind him.

Evelyn was waiting, purse on her knees and a smile on her face, always happy to see her son.

"Oh, Mama, I'm sorry to make you come out here this morning."

"Oh, it's no bother, Max. It's right on the way to church."

Max knew that wasn't true. Out the door in the already hot morning, they could hear the church bells blocks away.

"Oh, dear. We'll miss the processional."

"You go on, Mama. I can walk home from here."

"Oh, no you won't, *kleiner* Max. You will come along to church with me." She ran her eyes up and down her son's stained and wrinkled party clothes and back up to the old bruise on his forehead. "You are in dire need of forgiveness. And at the Zion Lutheran Church, we have an abundance of that."

• • •

Sunday was always family day at the Ritzi house, the day that Jock had his kids over. That was a fortunate thing from Max's perspective; with the ruckus of kids trampling the house, it would be easier for him to tiptoe around in the background. He'd come home with his mother after a long and agonizing church service. He'd washed up and fallen on the bed in his old room, exasperated and fatigued, but he'd been unable to nap.

He didn't come downstairs until late afternoon, when the house was full of the frisky screams and shouts of children being shooed out into the backyard. In the kitchen, the women were hard at work on the Sunday supper and not looking over their shoulders. No one was talking to each other, and everyone was avoiding eye contact. The tension inside that house was so thick, it could have been cut with a meat cleaver.

Max moved cautiously out onto the back patio, assuming that his father was parked in his dark corner, sucking oxygen and chewing on his cigars. He was wrong. As soon as he stepped out the door, he fell into the old man's line of fire.

"There is nothin', no amount a' God-fearing fathering, could ever alter the sinful nature of my own son!"

Ambushed. Someone had moved the old man out back, to the wicker rocker.

"The disgrace is mine. Damn you. Damn you! *Mein* own, *mein* own, always the drunken boy down in the jailhouse." He stood up easily, without remembering how frail he was, and stepped toward Max, raising his cane. "With all dis carousin' about an' alcohol and workin' the good girls of this town into whores . . ." He raged, red-faced, veins pulsing in his neck, incoherent and off his meds.

Jock, across the yard tossing a baseball with his sons, stopped and watched, as did his kids. Evelyn's and Gerdie's faces popped into the frame of the kitchen window.

"I'm not in the mood. You go find yourself someone else to pick on."

Maximilian was stiff, and his son's words never reached him. "I been wasting this whole life of mine in prayer, all to achieve redemption in your soul. Never mine. Hear, me? *Your* soul . . ."

"You tend your own damn redemption, Papa. I'll take care of mine. The ugliness in your life is not my fault."

The old man roared even louder. "I have searched. I have prayed. No way in hell to beat the sins out from my own son." He was spitting and dribbling on himself and stepping closer to Max, who didn't budge. Gerdie was on her way with a dishtowel.

"You!" Maximilian raised his cane and pointed at Max's face. Gerdie stopped just behind Max, her eyes wide and mouth agape.

"*Sie sind mein größter Ausfall!*" the old man roared.

"You can wallow in your own hell. You just keep me out of it." Max shoved the cane aside. "You keep Mama out of it, and my sister and brother, too. Don't you lay your phony righteousness on any of us!"

Maximilian's aluminum cane dropped to the ground with a low ringing sound. Gerdie stepped forward as if to intervene, but no words came out of her mouth.

Out in the yard a young voice taunted, "Aww. Uncle Max is gonna get his head cut in." Jock threw a hand across his son's mouth, but it was too late. All the boys were giggling loud enough for the two Maxes to hear.

Maximilian turned to the lawn and yelled to them all. He walked upright and steadily toward them, full of spunk and bile. "I have a rod for each and every one of you sinners. A rod you'll remember, by *Gott im Himmel.*" He stepped forward and took a wild swing with his left arm in the general direction of the boys in the yard.

Staggering off balance, the old man bumped against an ornamental glass lantern that shattered on the patio floor. He started to tumble down after it, his hands set out to break the fall.

Max reached out to catch his father. His hands grabbed the old man's denim shirt and held him there in midair, slumped but not fallen. Everything froze in that moment, and a sinister silence fell: Gerdie, still with the dishtowel. Jock and his kids in a motionless freeze tag out on the lawn. Maximilian sagging in Max's fists, gasping for air.

Gerdie rushed in to encourage her father back to his chair. "*Opa*, I think you should . . ."

Max left the ladies to fret over the *opa* and went back up to the room that was once his.

After a while Gerdie came up to see him in the kids' bedroom, staring at her brother and bottling her feelings as she always did, like a nurse with bad news. "Let's just keep things calm, Max. He's very upset right now." She took a position with crossed arms as she watched her brother shove clothes into his duffel. "You're right, you know. Our father can get ugly. And prone to outbursts." Her chin quivered. "Some irrational outbursts."

Max mocked her innocence. "And he likes to gouge the eyes out of little kitties, but other than that—"

"Stop that, Max! I'm surprised at you."

Max let out a loud breath. "My fight is not with you, Gerdie."

Gerdie's words were insistent and direct. "You need to find your way into a balance with him."

"This *is* balance, Gerdie. I've lived my whole damn life trying to duck him. I'm not doing that anymore."

"I know. I know." Gerdie stepped closer to him, the palms of her hands raised in concession. "We're a family, Max. We must love each other."

"That's just it, Gerdie. There will be no love in this family until he's dead." Max stopped his packing and sat on the bed. "You can choose to live with his abuse. I am choosing not to."

"You haven't tried, Max. You ran away."

His sister's words infuriated him. "I didn't want to leave! I was run out."

She backed off. "I didn't mean that in a bad way."

Max threw a handful of clothes onto the floor. "Do you really want your children living with him? Do you want them to grow up thinking that kind of behavior is okay? What kind of mother are you, Gerdie?"

The ferocious look in Gerdie's eyes scared him. "Don't you . . . !" She stepped closer and held a finger right up in his face. "Don't you ever tell *me* how to be a mother! Don't *you* tell *me* how to raise a child!" Max braced himself for a slap in the face. But Gerdie dropped her finger and stepped away. "That is something *you* know nothing about."

Max watched his sister move toward the door, but she stopped and put a hand to her face.

"Sure, it's mostly his fault," she murmured. "But it's your relationship with him that keeps the whole family out of balance."

Max shook his head and went back to shoving gear into his duffel. "This family does a lot better when I'm out of the way. You all just bask in the old man's sickness."

"We're not a family if you're not here, Max. And we're not a family without *opa*." She came back to the bed and paused before sitting down next to her brother. "You don't pick your family. God does. And He does it for a reason."

"Don't go all gospel on me, Gerdie." He stood and closed the straps on his bag. "I've had enough goddamn lectures."

She hesitated, then struggled to speak calmly. "I went out in the world too, Max. Both my kids were born in San Antonio. It was so crowded all the time, and so lonely all the time. And the gangs . . . It was bad, Max. It was bad out there." She paused. "We don't have that here in Fredericksburg. Do you think it was easy leaving my husband? I left him and came back because I wanted my children to grow up in a real family, in a real town. Not some nuclear family in an anonymous apartment somewhere."

"Do you really think your kids are safe *here*?" Max watched his sister gasp at the offense.

Rather than answer him, she stood to leave, but she turned back before reaching the door. "So your choice is to come back and be a burden to your father in his waning days."

Max crossed the room to his sister. "*You* are his burden, Gerdie. Not me. You are the ones keeping him sick. Treating him like he's an invalid." He saw how those words frightened her—the way that their father frightened all of them. He stepped back and tried to calm his tone. "He's not an invalid, Gerdie. It's the way he plays you. He's a cruel old man. And you keep him that way."

Gerdie closed her eyes when she heard that, as if to keep her chin from quivering. When she spoke, it was slowly and with great effort. "I am trying to deal with you as a brother, Max. But I am angry with you. And right now, I wish that you had stayed in New Mexico."

Max's shoulders dropped in despair. "I wasn't in New Mexico. I was in Arizona."

"You weren't here." In one fluid motion she spun on her heels, left the room, and slammed the door hard behind her. That was another Ritzi trait, to slam doors and stomp off before things were settled.

Outside, Max was embarrassed to find himself stranded, standing on the front porch with his laptop and his duffel bag. Trapped. Just like he was as a young kid without a driver's license, unable to get far enough away. He hadn't thought this through.

He dialed a number on his cell phone and caught Aubrey

at his house, watching the Rangers game with a few friends. Aubrey told Max that he was welcome to stay at the ranch, that he could help with some fencing that needed getting done. "Be down to get you right after the game, *mein alter Freund*."

Max was left sitting on the porch steps of the house he'd grown up in—no car, no way to get on the road.

• • •

Early the following week, after two hot days of pulling barbed wire at the Weshausens' ranch, Max got a ride back into town so he could pick up his car. He had received a curt call from Jock, telling him his car was all fixed up and asking him to pick it up quickly, claiming that he needed space in his shop. At Ritzi Agricultural Equipment, Max found his Challenger coupe as fine as it was when it came off the assembly line. A perfect paint match. They had replaced the fenders and smoothed out the rocker panels; great old German craftsmanship executed with imported Mexican artistry.

Max sought out his brother and approached him jovially. "This is great work, Jock. How the hell did you match that color? This is so good, I don't know if I can afford this. Where's the bill?"

"No. No charge for you, bro-brother," Jock addressed him stiffly. "You get the family rate." He paused for a stutter that didn't come. "Even if you don't get it."

"What about parts? And the paint? You had to cash out for parts, didn't you?"

"No charge, Max, but I need the bay, so you need to get it out of here. Like, right now."

Max looked around the shop. There was no bay—it was a large, open space with plenty of room for more vehicles.

"One more thing. No warranty. Take it as is, and don't bring it back." Jock turned and crossed the shop, heading back toward his office.

Max watched Jock's back as he walked away. Even shunned, Max felt a pang of respect for his little brother. He'd never known Jock to take such a strong stand on anything.

The Sin That Transcends Generations

Race days were always dress-up days for Mr. and Mrs. Carel Geische. Carel pushed himself into the stiffest of his pressed Wranglers and pulled on his ostrich-skin Luccheses, while Cora Lynn matched up her red cowboy boots with a lightweight bandanna-red dress. A lipstick smile curled up from beneath her big sunglasses as she moved through the crowds at the Gillespie County Fairgrounds. This was the movie scene that Carel relished—striding into a gunfight, outnumbered and outgunned. Time for him to stand tall.

"Now don't you go talkin' business an' all," Cora Lynn cautioned him as they climbed into the grandstands. "This is a social occasion. We're just gettin' to be friends with the new owners. Don't you go spoilin' that."

While seizing his accounts and rifling through his assets these Houston moneymen found that they now owned a box of reserved seats at the racetrack. The seats, parceled out to companies that made large donations to the Gillespie County Scholarship Fund, were simple enough: a clutch of metal folding chairs railed off on the second tier, overlooking the finish line. With unflinching determination, and with his charming wife at his side, Carel walked in as if he still owned them.

Schrubb introduced him to the several *auslanders* who now owned Geische Land & Development: Real Estate with handshakes and insincere smiles all around. "Howard Vader, our senior director from Houston," Schrubb mumbled.

Trying to remain polite, Carel had to choke back his contempt for the Houston men in their polo shirts and golf pants and the ladies in their silly race-day hats.

"Beautiful country you have here," Vader said without making eye contact. "In the past, I've only been here for the deer season." Vader was as cold as he was tall—not one who was comfortable with a smile.

"Well, sir, now you get to experience the hot side of the Hill Country." Carel got no immediate response from the Houston man. "How long are you going to be here, Howard? Or do they call you Howie?"

Vader looked him over disdainfully. "'Mr. Vader' will be fine."

"Just so happens my company has a hunting lease out on Ranger Creek." Carel put a special emphasis on the last two words and moved in closer to Vader. "Hogs are always in season up here. Maybe you and I should get out there and shoot some while you're up here."

Nose first, Vader turned to him and spoke quite clearly. "You no longer have a company, Mr. Geische." In a mechanical manner, he returned his attention to the track. "I am sure our branch manager has made that clear to you."

A hard man, Carel realized, but he didn't step away. "I

understand that, Mr. Vader. While you're here, we'll have to find some time to put our heads together about Ranger Creek."

The moneyman focused his attention on the line of horses making their slow walk to the starting gate.

"You'll need to do that," Carel insisted.

Schrubb elbowed his way between the two men, pushing a smile and cocking his head in a way that suggested Carel should back off.

Carel ducked around his old classmate's gesture. "I'm the one who knows how to pull this off. I'm the local boy."

Vader turned back to Carel. "We have our minds made up, Mr. Geische. We are not involved with you any longer."

"Yes, Carel. Let's just enjoy the horses." Schrubb turned to Cora Lynn. "Have you any bets on this race?"

Carel was disgusted to see how old Chuckie had cowered under Vader's hand. He saw himself as a lot more Texan than that.

"Look here, Howard, if you go and quit now, then you've just lost your ass on Ranger Creek. Stay in, and y'all can make something out of it."

A commotion at the starting gate had Vader's attention. Some jumpy quarter horse was bucking his handlers and refusing to load.

"Howie, I can see that you're not the player who would leave so much money on the table when he still has cards in his hand."

That drew Vader back into the conversation. "You've got grit, Mr. Geische. I like that in a man." He put his binoculars to his eyes and turned his attention to the starting gate. "However, you have neither the depth nor the history to pull this off."

The starting gun fired. An explosion of raw animal energy shook the ground. At once, everyone in the stands was on their feet, yelling as the horses pounded down the short track. All conversation was drowned by the call of the race, the strain of the crowd, and then the surge of frothy quarter horses crossing the finish line.

As the dust off the track was settling, it was Carel's voice that remained loud enough to draw the attention of those in the boxes on either side. "Come on, Howard. I've done all the shit work up here. Four years of playing your game, and I'll be damned if I'll let your little whining branch manager here screw it up!"

"Mr. Geische." Vader had only to cock his head away from his binoculars to stop Carel with the hard edge of his quiet power. "Please remember that you are a guest in my box."

A soft hand fell on Carel's shoulder, and Cora Lynn's low, honeyed voice said, "Oh, Carel, darling, let's you and me go downstairs and place some bets." She took his elbow and led him out of the box.

Reaching the top of the stairs, she stopped and spoke under her breath. "You are shaming me in public, Carel. Between your drinking and your"—she shook her head to come up with the word—"your little tantrums here."

Carel spun on her, his body blocking her at the rail, trapping her movement. "Do you know what these guys are doing? Do you know what these guys are doing to you?"

Folks on the stairs, neighbors and people they knew, eyed them with concern and seemed ready to step in between them if need be. But Cora Lynn wasn't the kind that needed rescuing. She slipped out from under his arm and tromped off down the stairs.

"Whose side are you on, Cora Lynn?" Carel started after her, hollering for all to hear. "Who was it that dragged you out of that trailer park and put you in Geische Manor?"

Cora Lynn kept a determined stride—not quite a run—out of the grandstands, through the food stalls, and past the crowd at the beer stands, all the way out to the parking lot, with Carel yapping along behind her and ending his rant only when they reached their truck.

"Damn it, Cora Lynn. Those bastards are trying to take everything we worked for." He smacked his hand on the hood, hard enough to bruise some fingers and cause Cora Lynn to flinch. "That lien I have on Mari's house is in that package too. It's not just us. They're going to take that away too. These guys are heartless."

He watched as she reached up, opened the door, and climbed into the driver's seat. His seat.

"I'm not really concerned about your ex-wife at this moment, Carel." Seated above him now, she spoke to him in a measured tone. "You and your conniption fits . . . I can't even show my face in public anymore."

Carel kicked his feet in the dust and shouted back, "Well, damn it all! You just get out of my truck." He lurched toward her, but Cora Lynn pulled the door closed in his face. He kept his thumb on the door latch, frustrating her efforts to lock him out. With one mighty heave, he jerked the door open, bringing Cora Lynn tumbling forward with a puny scream.

She shoved back at him, but instead of moving him away, the motion threw her back into the seat. "Get away from me, Carel!" She bent down and bit into his forearm.

He howled and fought back an urge to hit her. Instead he took a step back and stood his ground. "You think I'm going to stand for this? I'm Carel Geische, damn it."

She slammed the door and locked him out.

"You got nothing without me." His fists pounded the window as she started the engine. "You can't run out on me!" He winced as the gears ground painfully into reverse, then slammed into drive.

Cora Lynn glared down on him one more time. Then she left him in a cloud of fairground dust.

"Damn it, woman!" Carel bellowed. "That's not even my truck anymore."

• • •

Although he'd sworn he would never go back to that house again, a simple call from his mother was all it took to lure Max back into the family fold. "We will be going to the fair, a family in full," she declared. "All the grandchildren want a ride in your hot rod, so you will have to be at the house promptly at noon, my *kleiner* Max. Will they all fit in your car?"

My hot rod? Max silently reveled in the image of the cool uncle. "Yeah. I can squeeze them all in."

"Do you have seat belts for each and every one? All five of them are hankering to ride with you."

"Sure," he fibbed. "They'll be in good hands."

Here he was, being manipulated by his family once again. He'd been staying at the Weshausens' ranch, earning his keep doing farm chores and running into town with his laptop to use the free wireless at the public library, checking on his network marketing sales. His plans were to join Aubrey and Addy at the fairgrounds, but at his mother's gentle insistence he found himself back at his parents' house on Saturday—promptly at noon, as instructed.

As usual, the old man was a problem. The more the women fussed over him, the more cantankerous he became. He just kept carping at them: hassling about his wheelchair, complaining he didn't want that hat, barking at them about the oxygen canister. Nothing they did could suit him.

Max did not interfere. There was no way to apply common sense to either side of this game. Neither his sister nor his brother would have put up with this kind of behavior from their own children, but this—actually taking Maximilian out of the house—was a big deal for them.

On the way out the door Gerdie gave Max the portable oxygen kit. "You put this in your car."

"So, I guess we're talking again?"

"Just don't let him know you have it."

At the fairgrounds they set up their chairs on the ground level, in the shade, not far from the betting windows and just a few strides from the racetrack rail. Out there in public, the old man showed himself to be downright amiable among his old friends, longtime customers, past employees, and neighbors, who stopped by to visit with him, speculate about horses, and offer him a beer. Gerdie fended off the first few beer offers, but Maximilian finally took one from an old ranching buddy. The *opa* seemed to get a mean little pleasure out of the way his wife and daughter disapproved.

The Gillespie County Fair had its stock shows, its tarnished carnival rides, its simple country pageantry, and its band concerts, and there had been races there as long as there had been Germans in the county. The old guys talked about the horses that had been run in the middle of town, at the Marktplatz, until the houses and shops grew up too densely around it. Maximilian and his old geezer buddies cracked jokes and ranted about how, back in their day, the fair was a stock show that had some true meaning to the ranching families 'round here. "*Ach*, now all the *auslanders* just comin' here for that rock-and-roll show."

This was a side of his father that Max never saw: a jovial guy grousing and joking with his *alte Freunde* in their sing-song German.

Jock and Terri herded the children off toward the rusty old rides and doled out money for the carnival games down on the midway. With his father laughing among his old friends, and his mother and sister there to hover over him, Max slipped off to evade the tension that always seemed to well up when he was with his family.

They jumped him from behind while he was strolling past the concession stands. His old line—Heinie, Rickie, and Buddy—fell on him all at once, joshing around him like teenage pranksters while balancing plastic glasses of foamy lager.

"So, how you gettin' on with your new girlfriend?"

"Haven't seen you around much since you went out a-dancin' with Thea."

"And don't ya still have an out-of-state wife? You old dog."

"There is nothing going on between me and Thea," Max protested with an unconvincing grin. "Y'all talking like you never got past junior varsity."

"Not yet." They laughed.

"Hey, Road Trip. Get yourself a cold one." Rickie pressed a couple beer tokens into his hand.

Buddy threw his long arm around Max's shoulder, and the rest of the gang closed in and mustered him over to the tap line, under a sign that read CASH TRANSACTONS PROHIBITED. A crew of volunteers from the livestock association danced back and forth between the keg works and the long window where patrons paid for their beer with red tokens.

Hot sun, cold beer: a combination to guarantee an evening headache. With a glass in each of their hands, the jolly foursome ambled away from the concession stands toward the band shell.

"Band shell?"

"Yeah." Buddy nodded eagerly. "Nobody back there now. We're gonna burn a little homegrown."

"What?" Max stopped. "You guys still getting stoned?"

"Sure, dude." Heinie gave him a smile and cocked his head. "It's like a tradition with us."

"It's killer weed, Road Trip," said Buddy. "We grow it out at—"

"Oh, I don't need to know that." Max put up his hands to cut him off. *Who are these guys?* he asked himself. *Did I come back to get stuck in . . . what, some juvenile high school tradition?*

"Y'all go ahead." He motioned with his thumb over his shoulder. "I got to keep an eye on my dad."

• • •

Back at the family cluster, Maximilian had spit up some beer and was having little hacking fits. Gerdie labored over him with a handkerchief as Evelyn frantically fanned him with a racing program. With too many hands fussing over him, Maximilian shoved the women away in a weak but baleful manner. The man's old chums stood back with concern, and all this activity attracted a crowd of gawkers, which, it occurred to Max, was exactly the spectacle that Maximilian wanted to avoid.

"We need to get him home." Gerdie looked up at Max with the desperate eyes of a medic who was about to lose a patient.

"I've got that portable oxygen tank in my car. I'll pull up right behind the stands over there." Without awaiting a response, Max went for his car and returned, pulling his newly repainted, pitch-black Challenger coupe through the gate and up by the grandstands—drawing even more attention to the family fuss.

With considerable effort they got Maximilian into the front seat of Max's two-door coupe. When the old man was seatbelted into the front seat and sucking in deep draws of oxygen, Max pulled away from the mob of onlookers and drove out of the fairgrounds. The car's air conditioner struggled to cool against the stifling August heat. As they turned out of the fair traffic onto Tivydale Road, father and son found themselves suddenly alone with each other for the first time since Max had come home.

Maximilian pulled the oxygen away from his face. "Dat was an embarrassment, for sure. All dose people just gawkin' on. What were they thinkin'? An' what ya doin' driving right up? Show off your pretty black hot rod. *Gott im Himmel*, son. Ya got no brains?"

"Hey, you owe me, Papa. I got you out of there."

At the hard left turn onto the highway, the old man's stomach started to heave. He looked like he was getting ready to blow his lunch all over the car seats.

"Oh, Jesus, man. Not in my car. I just got it out of the shop." Max started reaching around for something to mop up with. The car swerved.

"Now, there ya go. Takin' the Lord's name . . ." Maximilian was choked off by the phlegm in his throat.

Max found a T-shirt behind the seat and pressed it harshly to his father's face while working to keep his car on the road. A truck behind them honked. Maximilian pushed the T-shirt back at Max, who swerved back into his lane and ran through a yellow caution light.

Along with spittle, Maximilian spewed unintelligible expletives about his son's "*Gott* damn" driving.

"Just keep your head out the window, Papa. I can pull over up here. Do you need me to pull over?"

Maximilian wiped his mouth on his sleeve and spit on the floor in disgust. "Don' you worry here, son. I'm not gonna soil your valuable car."

"It's not just a car. It's a Dodge Challenger, Papa. A classic coupe." He wheeled into another left-hand turn. "And I just got it cleaned."

At the house, Max let his father make his own way up the porch steps—a feat the old man was fully capable of performing on his own. Like a tired old dog going to his kennel, Maximilian found his way to the La-Z-Boy in the dark corner where Evelyn and Gerdie kept him. Max switched on the oxygen condenser that was parked behind the chair and placed the nasal cannula in his father's bony hand. If the old man needed oxygen, he could stick that tube in his nose all by himself.

A cave-like quiet filled the space as the walls squeezed in on the two of them. Maximilian's right hand crawled over to his Bible and his head tilted up to the ceiling, and from his mouth came fragments of what sounded like scripture, gurgled out between the steady pulses of the oxygen condenser. Sharp spasms lurched through his shoulders. Maybe Jock was right: Max hadn't been around enough to know whether this was run-of-the-mill dementia or a medical emergency. It would be just his luck to have the old guy pop off on his watch.

His father was drawing hard on his oxygen and bent so far forward that Max feared he would topple onto the floor. The old man's face was puckered up in its loose flesh, tears tracing down the weather-worn crevices of his cheeks. Those weren't body spasms. The old man was crying.

"Papa?" Max laid an easy hand on Maximilian's trembling knee. "Are you okay?"

"Sinner!" the old man roared. "A sinner, *Ich erzähle Sie!*"

Max was blown back by the spray of his words. "Christ! You scared the crap out of me." He had to shake himself to regain his wits.

Instead of tumbling to his death, the old man leveled his eyes on his son. It was as if the old man had suddenly come back to earth. "I, too, son. That old turkey buzzard stands upon my chest, too."

Those words caught Max like a hook. A chilly curiosity ran through his body, a simple, inexplicable fear. *What does this guy know?*

Stifling his anxiety, Max dragged a chair up to his father, the ladder-back chair his mother kept next to the kitchen doorway. He sat himself directly in front of the old man, within an arm's reach, and leaned forward as if he were speaking to a child. "What turkey buzzard is that, Papa? What is it that you saw?"

Maximilian sank back inside of himself, his head jiggling in a slow palsy. Words seemed to struggle in his mouth, like they wanted to come out against his will. The gnarled fingers of his right hand stroked the cover of his Bible as if he were petting a cat. It was eerie, something that Max imagined a spiritual possession might look like. Max had never seen anyone die. He braced himself to hear his old man's last words. *Where's Gerdie? Where's Mom?* They'd be the ones who would want to hear them. *Not me.*

The old man's eyes lifted upwards to fetch a memory. There was a quiver in his body, a rolling under his skin. The old man started to babble and drool, then his breathing calmed and Max could make out his words.

"Dat be *mein* own fault dat sat dat curse down on yer chest, my son."

Max realized that his words were meant for him alone. No

one else knew about the recurring nightmares of his darker days. "The turkey buzzards, you mean?"

His father's weathered eyes came back to his son. He raged up once again. "You! You."

This was the familiar side of his father—the raving Lutheran mystic. As crazed as the man could be, this was the more predictable personality. Max neither flinched nor responded.

"My name in de next generation." His hand was off the Bible and stabbing toward Max's face. "Where Gertrude gets my house and Jochiem takes my business, you . . ." He took in a deep breath. "You, *kleiner* Max, you will carry my sin. Forever. To eternity. And on to your own."

I came home for this bunk? The old man's threat left Max unimpressed. "Yeah? And who gets the turkey buzzards?"

"No joke! This is a sin, *Verdammt*. A sin saddled on you." His eyes rolled back, fogged over as he lapsed into the language he had grown up with: ". . . *immer Pferde jagen . . . Bullenreiten . . .*" Max picked out random words: horses, rough stock to be broke, rodeo buddies, and Mexico. His father kept saying *Mexiko*.

Everyone knew of Maximilian's younger days as a rodeo man. Max never doubted the old man's toughness. Odd, though, that his father had never displayed his championship belt buckles or showed any old rodeo photos. Carel had one from Uncle Victor. Max recalled that Mari kept a set of her father's buckles mounted for display on her bookshelf. He made a mental note now, that he should probably get one of his own father's buckles before the old man passed away.

"It's no sin to have a good ride, Papa."

"*Ach*." The old man shook his head, and the German words that followed were mostly lost on Max. "*Enge Freunde*, we were. *Drei schmutzige Kameraden*."

Good friends? Three . . . something friends. Dirty friends?
"Oh, don't go German on me," Max said, trying to keep his temper under control. "Just say whatever it is you're trying to tell me. And say it in English, for God's sake."

The angel of clarity settled upon Maximilian. The focus returned to his eyes, and he spoke without obstruction or temper. "Okay den. What happened. Down in Mexico a good ways back den. We lay de sin of fornication upon dat one Mexican girl. Each of us. Lord, each and every one of us."

Max's jaw dropped.

Maximilian went quiet.

Was that all he had to say? An odd sense of relief seeped through Max. He pursed his lips to keep a smile from creeping across his face. This was almost comical. His father went a-whoring down in Mexico. That almost brought out a human side of the old man.

"So, did you guys pay her for this? That happens all the time, you know." It suddenly occurred to him that this might have been something more vicious. "Or was this . . . uh, forced on her, like a . . ."

That brought the madman back out. "*Es ist egal,* boy!" he exploded. "It's a sin. Fornication is a sin, an' you . . ." He aimed a bony finger at Max's face. "An' you . . ."

"Oh, don't you go lay this on me." It was Max's turn to fly off the handle—so similar to his father's behavior. He caught himself, collected his thoughts, and continued in a calmer tone. "Let me guess. You and your old rodeo buddy, Victor Geische, the drunk. You said *Drei.* Three friends. Who was the third?"

The old man took a moment to stare into the past. "Teddy Hilss."

"Mari's father? Well, I never figured him to be the type."

"Teddy. *Ja. Ja.* It was Teddy. He was de one which goes back to get her. All de way back to Mexico."

"The Mexican whore?"

Maximilian looked back to his son. "*Ja,* he finds her. Wit' child. Pregnant by one of us. Or all of us." The old man appeared to laugh. "An' ol' Teddy goes an' marries her. Down here at St. Mary's Catholic Church. She has de baby right dere at de Hilss homestead." He gave his son a malicious grin. "Dey name de new baby for her Mexican grandmother, or something. Maribelle."

Mari Hilss? Did he hear that right? His father had spoken in English. There were no words to confuse. Max felt the blood drain from his head. "Mari? You could be the father of Mari?"

The old man's head was nodding. "Dat very person dat you copulated. De very one."

"My half-sister, then? Or Carel's, even!" The chair fell over when Max stood up. He struggled with an urge to strangle his father—to shove him to the floor and let his own feelings reign. "Well, damn you, then. Just . . . damn you!"

It was his father's turn to calm things down. "*Ja.* I am damned. Soon to start my time burnin' in de flames of hell for what I have done here on dis earth, in dat . . . dat *Gott verlassen* Mexico. An' I tell you now, I stand in fear of dat." He was climbing back into the pulpit now. "An' I'll have my own son dere to burn wit' me. Bathed in dose very same flames, not even to stop dere wit' you." He pounded out each syllable on the cover of his Bible. "*Dies ist das* sin that transcends all generations!"

Max saw it all now, like a specter creeping out from behind the blinds: how his father had wielded his guilt over them all— Max, his sister, and his brother—throughout their entire lives. If Maximilian had ever come to doubt the magnitude of that one sin, so long ago in Mexico, and all the consequences that had followed him home to Fredericksburg, then his own son's illicit sexual relationship with Ted Hilss's daughter had hammered home his belief once more. The tryst that drove Max out of town had provided his father with the confirmation of his own perverted theology—and driven the last undeniable nail into the old man's hell-bound coffin.

The front door opened. Evelyn and Gerdie were back, with reluctant children in tow. "The kids were getting tired."

"We were all getting overheated out there."

From his father's corner of the room, Max barely looked at them. Their figures seemed so gray, an abstraction. His jaw felt numb; his mind was racing. *Oh, jeez, half- or not! Not . . . my own sister.*

Maximilian's head tilted to the side.

"But maybe not my sister, though," Max whispered. "It could just as well be Carel, eh?"

The old man's breathing was slow and steady. The lids slid over his eyeballs like a reptile's.

Max reached out and shook his father's bony knee. "Wake up. Wake up, Papa."

Kids protested from across the room. "Why couldn't we stay longer?"

"Uncle Jock was there."

"We weren't tired, Mom."

"Hush." Gerdie silenced her boys and crossed the room to the dark corner, where her men were so covertly engaged.

Max stared blankly at her approach, as if he were in trouble. *My . . . sister?*

Maximilian, the coward that he was, had dozed off with the loose flesh of his cheeks bagging up on one side of his face, looking so fragile and innocent.

"It's okay, Max."

He recoiled when Gerdie's hand touched his shoulder.

"He's fine. Just napping."

Max's mind flashed uncontrollably on the years spent in condemnation of his father's rancid cruelty—and now there was more. *But me? Or Carel, even?*

He shook his head in revulsion. *What kind of pervert would fuck his sister?*

• • •

As daylight waned, the fairgrounds stretched out against the darkness. The outlying hills dropped into the edges of the night, while the neon lights and the skeleton frames of the amusement rides cranked their way up into the soft pink tissues of the fading skies. Whoops and hollers from the Tilt-A-Whirl rolled like a breaking wave over the hurdy-gurdy of the midway barkers and the whiff of deep-fried carnival food.

Carel had never missed a county fair in his life. Now he stood against a familiar rail, determined to set a new record for how many beers he could drink in one evening. The night crowd flowed in through the gates, heading toward the outdoor band shell, where a group dressed up like cowboys dragged their instruments and equipment out on the stage. The dance slab before them held a summer crowd of date-night romancers, gaggles of high school friends old and new, and real cowboys itching for a good ol' two-step.

Willow came waltzing through the gate on the arm of one of those Ebberhaus boys, wearing a smile as big as the moon. Seeing her there stripped the bitterness from Carel's heart. Just knowing that she was his daughter was better than all the money he had ever lost.

"But I don't have any money, and I don't have her," he said

to no one in particular. He decided to step up and say hello to her, maybe meet her guy, maybe become a bigger part of her life.

"Talking to someone?" Thea stepped in from his blind side and gave him a friendly hug. She was squeezed together and dressed to dance.

"No. I was just . . ." He shrugged. "Hey. You are looking pretty hot tonight. Can I get you a beer?"

Thea smiled at the flattery. "Save your money, Carel." Her eyes swept through the crowd. "I'm looking for Max. Have you seen him?"

The bitterness came back to his heart. He just shook his head to answer Thea and watched his daughter disappear into the dance crowd.

• • •

Max had buried himself in the anonymity of the dance crowd when Thea found him. She had a warmer greeting for him than for Carel, but it hardly registered. His mind was back in that sweltering living room, picking through the red-hot puzzle pieces that had spilled from his father's mouth.

When Thea took his hand, he was doused in a vivid recollection of Mari touching him. He recoiled as if snakebit before quickly apologizing. "Oh, sorry. I . . ." He forced a wobbly smile. "Caught me off guard."

"You pining for some other girl?" Thea joked.

He blew that off with a honey-toned "What would make you think that?" and a nervous laugh. He put his arm around Thea's shoulder and pulled her to his side so she wouldn't be looking at his face. It was at a dance just like this one where it all started going wrong with Mari. She was Carel's girl way back then.

The band started with some rocked-up country tune that

grabbed up the entire audience in one sudden beat. On the first chord, the minions became a pulsing sea in front of the stage. With arms stretched overhead they shouted the lyrics, while more traditional paired-up dancers scooted along the edges of the throng.

"You going to give me a dance, mister?" Thea asked with an unrefusable smile. "Looks like we have some cowboy-surfer music tonight." She wove her arm into his and lured him into a few simple steps.

Max remained distant—just going through the motions. He knew he wasn't the dance partner she'd discovered the other night. Over her shoulder, he spied Willow off in the crowd, dirty dancing with some muscled ranch boy. Willow's mother was out there too, ripping it up with some dark-haired stud. Max watched as mother and daughter caught each other's eye and exchanged a quick glance, some kind of signal or shared antic. They both smiled the same simple way.

My God, what they don't know.

"What?" Thea called to him, bringing him back to the girl in his arms. "Did you say something?"

He hoped not. "What do you say we get a drink?"

"Sure."

With a cool beer in his hand, Max made an effort to behave more like he was on a date. He smiled and nodded as Thea's mouth moved, but he didn't catch all her words—it was loud, and he was distracted. Then Thea was smiling and waving at someone over his shoulder.

Max turned to see Carel's fist on its way toward him.

He ducked, and Carel's arm wheeled through the air, connecting with nothing. Carel stumbled up again, getting in Max's face and shoving hard at his shoulders, splashing beer all over his shirt.

Those nearby took a step back, spontaneously forming an impromptu arena. Others pushed forward to bring on a fight crowd.

Max spoke first. "You . . . you got no idea what's going on here."

"Me?" Carel shrieked. "I don't know what? In my town? You're fucking with my people?" He pointed at Thea, who was stepping backwards. Then he pushed at Max.

Max held up his hand but Carel answered with another wide roundhouse swing, this one landing against Max's neck. The effort took Carel off balance and they fell into each other, grabbing and shoving and looking more like two bears dancing than a scuffle.

Max pushed him off. "Listen to me, dude. You don't know the truth about this. I do. You have no idea . . ."

Carel cocked his arm and threw it forward again, awkward. Max pulled aside. The force of Carel's own swing took him stumbling to the ground—first to his knees, then on all fours. It was ugly.

The crowd thickened around them. Max looked at his beer-stained shirt, then to Carel, who was getting up as awkwardly as a camel rising to its feet. Max took one step forward and kicked out, catching Carel below his ribs and rolling him back to the ground.

That's the way to settle this.

That blow gave Max a great sense of release, and he leaned in to deliver more, but a burly fair security man grabbed him from behind, one arm around his neck and the other pinning his right arm behind his back. Carel stood up on his own for a moment, then dropped back to his knees.

The moment froze like a photograph. No one moved. It became oddly quiet for a fair crowd—the music from the band shell became a muted background and the carnival sounded far, far away.

Carel raised his head. Standing over him in full uniform, with sunglasses dangling from his breast pocket, was Gillespie County Deputy Lester Metzger.

Lester stooped down in front of him and checked his breathing. "Think you've had enough fair for one night, Mr. Geische?"

Carel moaned something and rolled onto his side. Lester stood and nodded to the security man, who released his hold on Max. Lester's partner, Deputy Ortega, made his way onto the scene of the crime, squawking into his police radio. Max was certain that he was about to have another nasty meeting with the sheriff, but Lester said nothing while pulling Carel to his feet.

Willow and Mari were standing together, front and center where Max could hear them. "Why does Daddy have it out for Max so much?" Willow asked her mother. "I thought they were cousins."

Max turned to look at Mari, the childhood playmate who might be his half-sister, or maybe Carel's half-sister or cousin or something. She was rigid, chewing on her lower lip. Max remembered how she used to do that when they got into trouble.

The sin that transcends generations. The lies here were deep, so deep. No fight could resolve them.

"Tell her," Max barked at Mari. He nodded his head toward Willow. "Go on, tell her." He felt like he was about to cry or get sick. Or . . . something.

Nothing was said.

"Tell me what, Mom?"

Mari pulled her hair back and scrunched up her face like she had tasted something sour.

Out of the side of his eye, Max saw Carel shaking his head,

staring down Mari and telling her no. "Do you want her to hear it from me?" Max shouted at Carel. "Because, damn it, I will . . ."

Mari was slowly shaking her head. She turned to her daughter. "Well, Max is your father, sweetheart."

"Who?"

"Max. Max Ritzi."

"You're shitting me!"

"Willow, watch your language. You're out in the public." Mari paused.

"Max?"

"Yes. Your dad, Carel, didn't . . . well, biologically speaking, anyway. Carel Geische, well, yeah, he's the one I married. Acted like he was your father. Sometimes, that is."

Willow looked from one man to the other.

Mari pointed at Max. "And that fellow there . . . The only thing that he put into this deal was a small drop of his manhood."

Willow looked back to her mother and then to Max. Mari raised a finger and touched Willow's chin. "All he gave you was that little dimple you got right there. You ever notice that?"

Willow's laugh sounded fake. "You're kidding me, right?"

"The cat's out now, sweetheart. And we're done here."

"Really?" Willow seemed more quizzical than confused.

The crowd had meandered off to the next amusement. Thea was nowhere in sight. The lawmen held Carel off to one side, where he stood struggling to keep his balance and repeating, "I'm okay. I'm okay."

Willow looked back to her mother. "You know, I knew something was odd about this whole thing." She shrugged, looked at Max, and said, "Wow."

Max spoke directly to Willow, but his words were intended

for all. "I did you right, Willow. Secrets like that are going to screw you up in a big way. You can't even imagine what's going on here."

"Okay. That's cool." She didn't sound convinced.

Mari released a sigh loud enough for Max to hear, a big breath that she had probably held in for years.

Without waiting for Lester to come over and offer him first aid, Max turned and walked back into the anonymity of the fair crowd.

. . .

An ambiguous compulsion lured Carel onto Mari's front porch in the quiet of that deep night. He rapped on the screen door—not too hard, not too insistent. Waiting a moment, and mulling how wrong this might be, he knocked a second time. Waited. Then stepped away.

The night about him was set with stars. The moon laminated the hay stubble in the nearby pastures and drew a halo over the hills up there where Geische Manor stood. Cora Lynn had forgotten to shut off the patio light—something she never failed to do.

The door behind him opened, and Mari stood inside the screen, bedraggled and swallowed up in an oversized T-shirt. Neither angry nor disappointed, she looked as if she might have been expecting him.

"Is Willow here?"

"No." She cocked her thumb over her shoulder. "But Dean's here. You looking to get your ass kicked a second time tonight?"

I didn't lose that fight . . . The thought welled up from a corner of his mind but never made it to words. He almost said,

I'm sorry, but he wasn't sure where that fit in. So he went with, "I was just wondering about how Willow is taking all this."

Barefoot, Mari stepped out into the moonlight, closing the door softly behind her. "We best talk out here."

She took a seat at one end of the front porch glider. Carel stepped over and sat down at the opposite end.

"Whatever I did or didn't do," he proclaimed, "I kept your secret."

"My secret? Ha!"

Carel leaned in, trying to keep his voice down. "I'd never sell you out like that. Like Max did tonight. You know I'd—"

"You punched him in the face."

"Punch me. Go ahead. Kick me in the nuts. I'll still keep your secret."

"Quit." Mari shook her head. "It's all our secret. And it ain't no secret anymore."

Carel sat back and let the chorus of cicadas fill the silence between them. The glider bench squeaked a bit.

"You know I've been trying to get back to Willow."

Mari nodded—not like she believed him, but more like she was just listening to him.

"I know I have a lot of ground to cover, and I suspect tonight put an end to all that. Suspect I lost Willow for good. Wondering if you could—"

"What? Mr. Land and Development can't find a way to buy your way out of this one?"

"I got nothing, Mari. Stuck my neck out too far. This time the bank got it all."

She seemed to find that amusing. "Really? You?"

Carel nodded. "I'm dead broke. That truck isn't even mine anymore."

Mari was chuckling.

"What?"

"Well, you probably stand a better chance with Willow now."

He scrunched up his eyes.

"Money got in your way, Carel," she shot at him. "It wasn't just your daughter. An' me. Or even Max." She looked like she wanted to spit. "All you Geisches ain't nothin' but a bunch of goat farmers. Nothin' good happened when y'all had money. Just look at—"

"Okay." Carel held up his hands. "That's enough."

They stopped talking for a while, but they both knew they were not done.

Carel spoke up first. "You remember that note we took out on this place when I was just getting started?"

"I didn't do nothing. That was all you."

You signed it! he almost said, though it wasn't his place right now to be accusatory. "Well, the bank's got that, too."

She took a minute to digest that one. With the moon on her face, he could see her wince. "Oh, God in heaven, Carel. You taking me down with you?" Mari put her face in her hands, but Carel knew she was too tough to cry. She just sat there bent over, shaking her head.

He wanted to reach out to her, put his hand on her shoulder, reassure her, but he didn't dare. Most likely she'd throw a punch at him. And like she'd said, he didn't want to get his ass kicked a second time that night.

"Listen, Mari. I know this place is everything to you."

She raised her head to him, clear-eyed. "You ain't taking nothing from me, Mr. Geische. But Willow?" She threw a sarcastic laugh at him. "Some 'historical renovation' guy you turned out to be. Made a mess outta your daughter's own heritage." Then she got up and went back in her house.

Evening Prayers

"Well, I think I'm just going to have to burn this house down to the ground." Mari spoke with the offhanded tone she would use if she were going to plant some geraniums in the window box. Her old high school friend Chuck Schrubb had called from the bank, saying she would soon be kicked out of her house because she'd been so dang stupid back in the day, when Carel got her to sign off on that loan note so he could get his dang building company started up. "What on God's green earth was I thinking?"

But she knew what she was thinking at that time. She had a little baby to take care of, her dad was drooling himself to death in a nursing home, and she was just doing everything she could to keep her husband around. And trying to get rid of him, all at the same time.

"It's just the one dwelling and the lot it sits on," Chuck had told her on the phone. "The rest of the land and the other buildings are clear of any financial encumbrances. Your Sunday house and the outbuildings are not included in this deed of trust."

"Deed of what? It's *my* house, Chuck. It's where I was raised. It's where I raised up Willow. It's not some . . . whatever you called it."

"I know that, Mari. That's why I'm calling. I want to give you the first opportunity to pay off this loan. I know it looks like a lot of money, but I am willing to help you find terms that we both could work with. However, the bank will need to get a good down payment, and we would have to move quickly."

"Carel ain't got no money at all, then?"

"No, ma'am." Chuck's tone was apologetic. "The old Geische Land and Development company has nothing left."

"I wasn't askin' about his company, Chuck. I was trying to figure out if Carel could help out any."

Chuck let out a deep sigh, the kind that foreshadows bad news. "No, Mari. He's got nothing. My bank made certain of that."

• • •

Those one-hundred-degree days were full of accusations and foul tempers. Never before had Mari and Willow been so stuck with each other, languishing in the air-conditioning, making iced tea, and getting on each other's nerves. The heat stopped them from getting anything done, and unresolved issues hung over them like an unmade bed.

"Well, you're the one who fucked it up" was Willow's flat-out response.

"Language, please."

"I'm supposed to be getting married, stepping up to do my part in keeping this family going, and you, Mom . . ." She just balled up her fists and made a growling sound.

"Sweetheart, I was just—"

"You screwed up your marriage, that's one thing." Willow threw herself on the sofa. "And now you're screwing up mine!"

Cautiously, Mari sat herself on the sofa just out of Willow's reach. "Willow, darling, don't you worry about what happens to this house. If you love that boy, you go on and marry him."

Willow was shaking her head. "Love? Is that what you thought it was when you married my dad? Or when you were carrying on with my real dad? Whichever one was which."

"Am I supposed to have some excuse ready for that? I can't undo what's already been done, now can I?"

Willow was shaking her head. "It's never about love, Mom. It's like this now: I need a place to stay. That ain't love."

"If you're referring to your fiancé, sweetheart, it's a whole lot different. He's a fine catch for you, Miss Willow. Stable kind of boy from an old family in town, and a great body—I mean, like, a nice, muscled-up guy, a hardworking man." Mari reached forward, kissed two of her fingers, and then tenderly placed them on Willow's cheek. "But I didn't think I raised the kind of girl who would say yes to someone she didn't think she loved."

Willow winced and backed away from her. "Oh, Mama. How come nobody really gets it? Ryan is ambitious enough, but he ain't got nothin'. Soon as I say 'I do,' he's got himself this here farm an' you get to see my kids running down that back pasture to Palo Alto Creek down there. But nothin' like that is gonna happen now, is it? In Gillespie County, marriage is no different than a real estate deal."

Willow stood and walked upstairs to her room, the hottest room in the house, where Mari knew she would go through a slow-motion act of getting ready for an evening with Ryan. Blue jeans and a selection of tops would soon be strewn across her bed.

Mari wandered out onto the front porch for her evening prayers. That was Willow's term for the frequent occasions when her mother would sequester herself on that old porch glider—sometimes with a beer, sometimes with one of the trashy novels she was always reading, and sometimes with just her anxiety and her tears. But it would always be in the evening, and Willow always left her alone out there. Mari could spend hours out on that porch by herself, gnawing on her fingernails and mulling the things that she had no control over. On occasion she would be struck by some profound insight, and she'd go hunting down Willow to share her revelations. One time it was the color she'd chosen for the kitchen window curtains. Another time it was how to pay for the repairs on her old Jeep.

A little while later, Mari found Willow up in her room, sitting on the chair in front of her mirror in a T-shirt, brushing out her hair. "Mind if I come in?"

Willow just kind of shrugged her shoulders but said nothing as Mari moved aside some clothes and stretched herself across the unmade bed. Nothing was said for a long while. The Band-Aid was off Willow's ring finger, and the little pink scabs showed with every stroke of the brush. Each woman studied the reflection of the other's face in the mirror.

Mari broke first. "When I was just about where you are now," she started saying, "I was up here in this very same room." She paused. Willow's hairbrush did not miss a stroke. "It got all screwed up, right out of high school."

Willow turned to her. "You don't have to go digging through the past. I'm not one to be passing judgment on anything you might have done back in the day."

"It's not all about that 'back in the day' stuff. This is about you and me right now." Mari sat up on the side of the bed. "I can't see how you can come to understand your place here when I haven't been completely honest with you." She left another long pause, took a loud breath, and added, "That's what I realized just now."

"Evening prayers?" Willow muttered as she turned her face to the mirror and started to powder the shine from her cheeks. She kept a cold eye on her mother.

"If what happened . . . Anyway, who could you trust except . . . ? Well, the three of us had been such close friends growin' up. Carel, Max, and me. But that 'best friends forever' stuff, well, that changes when ya get older and get . . . horny, I guess. Changes all of us. Carel got to me first, and you know he don't let go of nothin'. And like you were sayin' downstairs, it had nothing to do with love and everything to do with needing to have something to own. Like property. Yes, we were a thing, and then there was Max left on the outside looking in. All hollow and empty, just like you seen him the other night."

Willow was studying her mom's face at the same time she was trying to apply a steady streak of eyeliner.

"We'd get to fighting, Carel and me, and we'd be kind of on again, off again. You always do, because you think it might be about love. Anyway, one time, when we was off again, Max smelled that blood in the water and came 'round for me. I let him. I welcomed it. I was glad for him at the time. One short night, at the exact right time of the month, you know? It wasn't even about me either. He just did it to get one up on Carel, and that split the whole thing wide open. The fight thing was just about them two horny bulls going right at it, but it ended up I was the one carryin' the baby. And that baby was you."

Mari wanted Willow to say something, but she didn't. Mari waited a moment before she continued.

"Then Carel . . . It was kinda queer. I thought he'd come back and beat me up or something. But he come back on his knees and begged to make an honest woman out of me." She gave a little forced laugh. "Carel wasn't doing it for *me*. Figured this part out much later. He just couldn't let Max get the last say. It all blew up like nothin' you ever seen. And that put Max Ritzi out on the road again. His old man found out, 'cause no one can keep a secret 'round here, and he was gonna kill him for it. So Max was on the run."

Willow had stopped with her makeup but still had nothing to say. The quiet pulled up around them like the August heat. Mari stood as if to leave, but instead she came over to Willow and messed a bit with her hair. Willow let her.

"Carel and me, we got married real quick. We had you. Tried to make it work, but what did we know? That one quick lay cast a long shadow over the whole thing, and we just couldn't get out from under it. 'Til now."

Mari ached for her daughter to say something, but Willow just sat there contemplating herself in the mirror, holding a lost, sullen look, like she'd just heard her biopsy came back positive.

Then Willow's chin dropped to her chest. "So that's what it's gonna be like for me." It wasn't a question.

Mari was startled. "What scares me most, sweetheart, is that all these little secrets—secrets and lies—have all come down on you." She reached out and took her daughter's hand, gently tracing the marks that marred Willow's ring finger, kissing them. "These are my scars too, sweetheart. I put them there just as much as you did."

"It's not like something I do all the time, Mom. Not like it's a hobby or something." Willow raised her face. "I don't have any control over it. It just happens."

"I know, I know," Mari said, as though soothing a child

who had just skinned her knee. "I don't care what you done—that's behind us." She paused and gave a smile. "Now, that sounds like something you were just saying to me, don't it?"

Willow pressed tight on her lips and bobbed her head.

"I really can't tell which one of us is raising the other anymore." Mari shrugged in surrender. Then she drew in a breath, collected herself, and said, "I better let you get cleaned up. You gotta start all over, and your beau's gonna be showin' up here pretty soon."

When Ryan's truck rumbled through their gate, it pulled a cloud of caliche dust up to the house. "Evening, ma'am. Hot enough for you?" A southern gentleman, he gave no hint of their encounter at the South Star the other night.

"You can call me Mari, Ryan. I'm too young for you to be ma'am-ing me." She was looking at him somewhat differently, trying to pierce that polite, good-looking veneer to see his devil's horns. "How's your *oma* getting on? Is she adjusting to her new home?"

"Yes, ma'am. Doin' well."

"You been calling on her regular?"

"Well, I been kind of—"

"It's hard moving into a nursing home. Your *oma* needs you, you know."

"Yeah. I hear ya. I'll be visiting with her after church this Sunday."

"You be sure to do that." Mari smiled coyly down upon him. "And do give her my regards."

"I will, ma'am. I mean, Mrs. Mari."

Mari imagined that he and Willow would be going out to do some dancing at Luckenbach, where the boys took her back in her day, then they would end up drinking way too much at the South Star, like she always had.

Willow came bounding onto the porch, all smiles and done up for the evening: ass-tight jeans, tank top, cowboy boots, and dangling from her neck, a silver cross she'd taken from Mari's jewelry box without asking. She had a fresh Band-Aid around the finger where Ryan hoped to see his engagement ring, and she brought with her a Shiner Bock fresh from the fridge, handing it to her mother.

"We're off, and don't you worry if we don't make it home tonight." Willow placed a kiss on Mari's forehead. "We're, you know, almost legal."

Willow slipped her arm through Ryan's and turned him toward his truck. Turning with her, Ryan spoke loud enough for Mari to hear. "I kinda like your mother."

At the truck, he held open the door for her, and she shot a glance back to Mari, still sitting in the porch glider with the cold beer in her hand, smiling. It was a mutual smile, Mari thought, that only a mother and daughter could translate.

The truck cruised down her long driveway toward the swelling lights of the town. Just out of spite, Mari called after them, "Don't lay my daughter tonight."

• • •

A kid goat stood on the hood of a white Honda Accord on the corner of Llano and Main streets, oblivious to all the honking and shooing going on around him. The Honda's driver had left his door wide open and was out in the street, waving his arms and imploring the dim animal to get off his car. His gesticulations only got the baby goat to prance up his windshield and hoof about on the roof. The driver slapped his forehead with both hands as he stomped in desperate little circles in the middle of the town's main intersection. Traffic was plugged up in all directions under a signal light that dutifully flashed from red to yellow to green and back to red, with no effect on the mayhem below.

The way Carel figured it, the Honda with out-of-state plates had right-turned into a pickup hauling a crate of pygmy goats, spilling them into the intersection.

A city cop was on his knees along with the goat owner, trying to cajole another kid out from under a delivery van. Caught up a block away, a Gillespie Country sheriff's car had left its lights flashing, and Deputy Ortega ran between the rows of stalled vehicles toward the scene, his right hand on his holster as he hollered into his walkie-talkie.

From the way the shoppers on the shady side of the street jumped back, Carel knew there must have been another goat running down the sidewalk. This was the first time he'd laughed since the bank had locked him out of his office.

Under his summer straw Resistol, and toting an overstuffed leather briefcase, he had come downtown to wrangle around with his former tax accountant. He now stood on the sidewalk with a crowd of rubberneckers who were enjoying the Main Street goat roundup.

An old friend of his Uncle Victor stopped when he saw Carel. "That'd be ol' man Lang's goats out there," the old crony volunteered. "That last big bang was that there white car smashin' into Lang's goat crate. I heard it all. Don't know where he is, but that's his wife out there workin' to get the kid out from underneath. Can't remember her name. Think it all started with that first truck up there."

Carel stepped into the street and marched up to the old Ford pickup, askew across two lanes, with the words *Geische Custom Framing* barely scraped off the door. Old man Lang's goat truck was embedded in its rear fender, and Willow sat in the driver's seat. She had just come from work—still wearing that old German dirndl and her hair pulled back.

"I was just going to the bank to cash my payroll check." She seemed to be apologizing to Carel, before switching to tattle-tale anger. "That asshole pulled out in front of me."

There was yet another car, pushed into the grill of Willow's truck. Steam from its smashed radiator hissed in the breeze. A city cop was there too, dutifully taking information from a short lady hidden behind a big straw beach hat and sunglasses that covered most of her face: the perpetrator of the whole mess.

Carel peeked around the front of the hood. "Looks like she got the worst of it. But you won't be able to drive this out of here." He turned back to see the fragility behind Willow's stony mask—her gathered brow and pursed lips. "You're going to be okay, sweetheart. Nothing here can't be fixed."

"It's the way my whole life's been going." She wasn't digging for his sympathy. "A complete goddamn wreck."

"Don't you worry, Willow. I'll take care of this. It will all work out."

"You?" Willow pulled the vehicle registration from the sun visor and opened the door. "All of it?" Her eyes accused him of everything as she stepped out, her long Bavarian dress falling almost to the street.

Stepping carefully around the hissing radiator, the police officer with her clipboard came around to the hood of the truck, followed by the beach-hat lady. Besides the sunglasses, the beach hat lady had on way too much lipstick. "Oh. I am so, so very sorry about all of this."

"All of this?" Willow handed her license and registration to the cop. "I ain't got no insurance. Couldn't afford none."

"Oh!" The beach-hat lady seemed offended.

"That's a ticketable offense in Texas," the female cop said

without looking up from her clipboard. "Are you the owner of this vehicle?"

"No. It's my dad's truck. Right here." Willow gestured to Carel and, turning to him, "We never got around to changing the title, neither."

My dad. Carel flushed for a moment—like he was embarrassed. Or proud. She still called him Dad. Everyone around him was fretting about the accident or chasing goats, and Carel stood amid the chaos, taken aback by the sudden surprise of fatherhood.

"I'm talking to you, sir." The police officer brought him back from his moment of bliss. "I need to see your driver's license."

"Oh, yes, ma'am." Carel whipped out his wallet and passed the card to her. "See here. The names are the same."

A look of suspicion rolled out from under her visor.

"Look here. We're both Geisches."

No one got a ticket for the car accident, but Carel got one for uninsured vehicle and another for expired plates. With two pygmy goats wrangled up and the other run off, tow trucks were called to haul off the cars that were insured. Mrs. Lang drove off with her goats and some new dents, leaving Carel and Willow standing there together, so ironically mismatched but so typically old Fredericksburg—a pressed-jeans cowboy and the St. Pauli Girl.

"I'll call Jock to fetch the truck. He's just down the street here."

"What? You think we got some farm stuff out here? He doesn't have a tow truck."

Carel was already dialing. "Yeah, but he's a ranch boy."

Sure enough, Jock Ritzi got there pretty quick, riding an old, well-worked John Deere tractor right down Main Street. The cops didn't like having to deal with a slow-moving farm tractor while they were trying to get the traffic moving again, but with the help of Carel and Deputy Ortega, they winched the front wheels of the truck up against the tractor. Looking more like a broken parade float, their handiwork attracted a group of tourists who snapped photos.

"Hey, Jock," Willow called out over the rumble of his tractor. "I'll get you paid for this, but I can't make it right now."

"Ah, don't worry about it. It's the family rate."

The old John Deere chugged off down the street, lugging the old truck behind, like some oversized worker ant heading back to its queen. It dragged its load around the corner, and the show was over.

Carel jerked his head. "Come on. I'll give you a ride home."

"It's not far. I can walk."

"Dressed like that? Everyone will stop you and expect you to fetch them a beer."

Willow smiled at that. "Yeah. Okay. You got a point there."

Carel held the door open and, gathering up her skirt, Willow climbed into the front seat. He wheeled out into the street, so incredibly aware of the mountains that stood between them. Nothing was said. No topic seemed safe.

Willow clung tightly to good manners, her eyes straight forward, fixed on nothing she hadn't seen all her life—holding it all in.

Carel thought, *And I did that to her.*

Willow reached up to her head with both hands and shook her hair loose. Maybe so she wouldn't seem so exposed to him. It took an effort not to stare at her. He choked on an urge to tell her how sorry he was, to explain his version of the story, but every word he thought of seemed false or insincere. The left turn onto Washington Street brought a knot into his stomach. What could he say?

The truck pulled up to the gate of the old Hilss farmstead.

"Just here is good." She turned her eyes to him. "You just might get shot at, drivin' up too close."

He wanted to think that was a joke, but he couldn't read her.

"Really," she said with a smirk.

"Well, I'd deserve that." He shrugged. "Listen. I know I've been awful in so many ways. There is so much I need to make up for. But the thing I botched up the most . . . The worst thing I ever did was not taking care of you."

She cocked her head like a curious puppy, studying him. He didn't know her well enough to read her feelings. She didn't seem bitter.

"I did a lot of people wrong, and I think I can make amends for some of it. Your mother's house, for instance." He winced. "But with you, Willow, and all the . . . Well, I don't know how to make that right. And I really want to. Somehow."

A tiny smile betrayed the softer side of Willow. She reached out and lay a hand on his forearm. "I can only imagine how fucked up things are for you right now. But I just got my paycheck cashed, and there are some people waiting on this money."

She jumped out of the truck, and Carel watched her tromp all the way to the front porch. She never looked back.

• • •

Max's fingers were quivering as he reached for the gate latch at the Altdorf Biergarten. That surprised him. *Nervous?* He was simply dropping by to visit with his daughter again—at their habitual time, in the late afternoon heat. After their fair night epiphany, she would be eager to hear him out. Or maybe not.

He took his usual seat under the veil of the oak tree at the far end of Willow's section and readied himself for the purpose of this visit. The one thing he could do, as a father, was spare her from the wad of family poison bundled up in—what did his father call it?—the "sin that transcends generations." She would understand that it was not his fault. So why should he be apprehensive?

She took her sweet time getting to him. Abandoned with his thoughts, Max wondered if she was deliberately avoiding him. He was patient for a while, then annoyed with her. Finally it occurred to him that whatever she was doing may be something he deserved. Any other customer would have walked out.

Finally, she made her way to Max's table, bringing him a tall stein of Spaten Optimator.

"Sorry about the wait. I just had to get some stuff out of the way so we could talk." Willow scooped the skirt of her dirndl under her knees and took a seat in the chair next to him, close enough for a cozy chat but not so close that they would appear to whisper. "I'm on a break now."

She was nothing but a puzzle to Max. Now he realized that he'd had it wrong. She wasn't keeping her distance; she was allowing room for him.

"I thought you may want more of an explanation about the other night," he began, getting right to his mission with an unfamiliar paternal tone in his voice. "At the fair, I mean. It must have been something of a revelation to you."

"Nah." Willow stopped him with a shake of her head. "It's okay. Really. I'm cool with that."

"Did you know?"

"No. Not exactly." She shrugged and turned her soft eyes away from him. "Anyway, what does it matter now?"

Max let those words echo for a moment. "There's a lot more to it. It goes way back to things that went down with your grandfather, my dad, and Carel's Uncle Victor . . ."

He saw she was tuning out, glancing back at her tables and scanning the fence line for a distraction.

"It's not just me and Carel," he pressed on. "You need to know. It's a trap that could come around and bite you, Willow."

Her eyes came back to him, but she wasn't buying into his sense of urgency. "It's just a bunch of old stuff. I know what I'm doing. I'm going to be leaving all that here."

"You taking off?"

"Yeah. I know you probably came back here to catch up with your long-lost daughter and all." She changed courses on him again. "I wish I had more time with you. I really do. But it's time for me to blow this town."

The blend of sarcasm and sweetness in her tone tipped him off balance. "Well, good. I think that's a good thing." He forced an unconvincing chuckle and reached for his beer. "You'd probably expect that old Road Trip Ritzi would get behind that one."

At the same time he toasted her decision to leave, he was desperately aware that this may be his only chance to spill the family beans. He groped for the words that would take this conversation back. *She needs to know, right?*

She leaned into him. "I'm gonna let it all stop here. I'm not taking any of this with me."

Let it all stop here. He was beguiled. A little voice from way back in his head told him she was right, told him to just drop it. Just let her go. Did she really have to know?

What if the curse ended here?

"I got no problem with anything that went down way back when," she was saying, "The problem I got is with my truck. It's down at your brother's shop right now."

"Jock?"

She cracked at him for being so dopey. "Ya got any other brother I don't know about?"

181

"You never know in the families around here." He could see that she missed the irony in that remark.

He gulped down another mouthful and looked past Willow to a group of bikers coming into the beer garden, all decked out in leather even in the summer heat. Here, he realized, was where he could actually slip the grip of his father. He could put an absolute end to "the sin that transcends generations." He could reduce his old man to irrelevance just by keeping his own mouth shut. *Could it really be that simple?*

Willow's eyes bounced from thought to word as she spieled on about some tourist who had pulled out in front of her truck and how embarrassing that was. "I was, like, standing out in the middle of Main Street in this friggin' Halloween costume," she grumbled. That was when she saw it, she told him: She was going to either be penned up like Mrs. Lang's goats back there, or run off like that other one. "The one that got away," she explained.

Max watched her passions flow, although he wasn't quite following her story. He sipped on his Optimator and let the truths and sins that he had carried in with him slip into the dark crevices of his pocket, where they could be forgotten. Those nasty secrets could die right here.

In that same pocket, he found his car keys. "Well, if you're really getting out, take my car."

"What?"

"The Challenger. It suits you. You'll like it. Just get out there and get after things."

"Me, in your precious hot rod?" she taunted him. "You're shitting me."

He twisted the car key off his key ring. "Yeah. Look at it as your inheritance. It's the least I can do." He sat back and basked in the radiance of her grin. "You can take my place. Be the new Road Trip."

"What will you drive?"

"Aw, I'm back home now." He gave her a wry smile. "No one's going to take me seriously until I get a truck."

•   •   •

"They say they'll be more than happy to take me on at Crossing Creek Realty, so long as I bring along my listings." Cora Lynn was back and forth between the kitchen blender and the outside patio. She didn't stop talking when the door shut behind her.

Carel stood in the sun without a hat, watching heat waves shimmering off the town below, basking in an odd stillness. He didn't turn his head when his wife buzzed back onto the patio.

"Of course, the problem is that we had to give up them listing agreements to the bank. But if I got myself registered under another brokerage, I could still get the seller's side of the commission. Did I leave that paring knife out here? You know, the cute one we use for slicing up limes. I don't see it anywhere." And she was through the door again, her voice lost in the whir of the blender.

The pastures below were burnt and yellow. The sun ricocheted off the tin roof of the old Hilss farmstead, stinging Carel's eyes. He was remembering the summers he spent in that house before air-conditioning, when Cora Lynn walked into his daydream with a couple of salt-rimmed margarita glasses.

"It's too hot to be out here, sugar boots." She passed one to him. "Let's go inside."

He had come home early that afternoon to drop the latest

bombshell on her. But now, with her there, passing him a margarita glass, he could only say, "It's August, darlin'. It's supposed to be like this." Maybe this was not the right time to tell her.

She started talking about a hair appointment she had coming up, and how she might come home with a different look. "Just warning you ahead of time. You know how you hate surprises." She lured him over to sit at the shaded table that was just a tad cooler than standing out at the balcony rail.

Surprises? There would be no better time. When he found a gap in her words, Carel blurted, "I saw Vader and a bunch of his lawyers this afternoon."

"Did you show him your better manners this time?" She wrapped her words around a cute little smile.

Her wit charmed him, and he regretted opening this door, but still . . . "Yes, I did," he said with an artful chuckle.

"Well, did you get better results by behaving yourself?"

"As a matter of fact, I did." He nodded with a closed-lip grin. "I worked a pretty clever deal."

A hopeful Cora Lynn smiled for him to continue.

"I gave them this house in an even-steven exchange for the note on the Hilss place down there."

He watched her expression melt. "You don't mean Mari's place? We're not going to move down there."

"No. It's still Mari's. Willow's too, I guess. Now it's just"— he reached for the legal term—"unencumbered."

Cora Lynn stared at him like a stunned mullet.

He leaned toward her. "It was the right thing to do, darlin'. Her family's had that place since this town first started. To hand that farmstead over to a bunch of *auslanders* would be . . . well, a blow against the family traditions of this town."

"And you're givin' up our house for *that*?" She started to

rise out of her chair. "Did you put any thought into what we'd be doing? Did you think at all of talkin' to me about it?"

He stared hard at her. "You would have argued me out of it. It didn't require your signature. I owned it before—"

"Well you gotta get it back." Cora Lynn sat back down. "You have to undo this, Carel."

"Already got it signed, notarized, and sealed. It's done."

"God!" Cora Lynn shook her head and her hands like she was casting off evil spirits. "I raised my boys in this house!"

"I did think about you." His voice was thick with calm deliberation. "I thought about how you would feel if I'd gone and done something like that to you."

"You didn't do it to me. I don't care about your ex-wife!" Cora Lynn shot to her feet. "You're married to me now. And when you go and do stupid things like this . . . Well, we're both screwed. Damn it, Carel!"

"I didn't think you would want to be married to a man that could just take some property he didn't really own, someone who could go so far as to put a family out of their home. I didn't think you'd want to be married to someone like that, darlin'."

"Oh, don't you *darlin'* me."

He held her with a firm look. "And I don't want to be somebody like that."

She broke away from his gaze. "Was it Willow? Did she talk you into this? That little Jezebel is just working you!"

Carel flinched at that jab. He sipped at his margarita. "Willow doesn't even know."

Cora Lynn fumed across the patio, pulled open the kitchen door, and shot him a deadly stare. "I can get me a job with Crossing Creek Realty and find my own place to live. But I don't know what you're gonna do." The door swung closed behind her.

Carel stared at his unfinished margarita, thinking that there might have been a better way to go about that. *But . . . what the hell. I got it done.* He just hoped that she wasn't going downstairs to get one of his guns.

The door flew open a moment later, and Cora Lynn stepped out, unarmed. "You better go and make up a list of whatever we got left, mister. 'Cause you and me gonna be splittin' it right down the middle. Texas is a common-law marriage state."

Bam! The door slammed hard this time.

•   •   •

Then Carel had his sister to contend with. On the phone, Jeanie told Carel that she and her daughter were heading back to Austin. "Join us at Lincoln Street," she urged. "You can say good-bye to your niece and share a parting glass with me."

"Sure." His voice was amenable but not enthusiastic. "I'd like to see you all off, but I won't be able to contribute any juicy gossip about my wife walking out on me." He immediately realized those words were unfair to Cora Lynn. "I just don't have any answers."

"Why, big brother, do you think I'd be fishing for gossip?"

"Because it's you. And because there is wine involved."

"It's where we live. There's always wine involved."

"Just don't go away blaming everything on her."

"Oh. I never assumed it was her. I grew up with you, remember?"

Thea and Gerdie were sitting with his sister under the arbors at Lincoln Street when Carel walked in. That pissed him off. He was hoping for some one-on-one time with Jeanie, not a public dissection of his recent woes. His disappointment was quickly disguised when his niece ran to him, hugging her cheek against his thigh and squealing, "Uncle Carel! Uncle Carel! Mommy's friend gave me a new kitten for going away."

The kitten was a knit sock that fit over her hand and had buttons for eyes. Carel knelt to Caitlin, tugged on the puppet's ears, and cooed with the child while shooting disparaging glances at his sister. For their part, the klatch of magpies smiled approvingly from behind their wine glasses at the uncle-niece playtime, without so much as a change in the pitch of their mile-a-minute chitchat.

A moment later, Carel acquiesced to the seat they had saved for him and pulled Caitlin onto his lap. A wine glass was set out for him and, without the slightest pause in whatever she was saying, Jeanie reached over to pour out a thin pink rosé. Carel held up his hand and shook his head. As the ladies gushed on, Carel silly-talked with his niece, who pushed the kitten puppet into his face whenever his attention strayed to others at the table.

Their eager topic was Thea, who had met a man through an online dating service—a recently divorced guy from an Austin suburb. "So, we'll be seeing a lot more of you in the city," they laughed.

"I've thrown in the towel on the local dudes," Thea told them, explaining that she had reached out to the Internet for something she hoped would be more . . . well, whatever it was that she was looking for.

"Ah, yes," the other ladies emoted, casting their blameful eyes to the local man at the table.

Carel knew they would soon be inventing stories about him and Cora Lynn—stories that started with *After all he's done for her*, or maybe *He never deserved her* or *I can't believe how he screwed her over*. The rosé nudged their fanciful prattle toward viciousness.

Carel ordered a beer, one of those stylish ones in a designer bottle, made by monks in Europe. Those bottles were smaller and the beer more bitter—flavorful, but not made for drinking on a hot day. You couldn't get a Lone Star these days at chic wine bars like the one on Lincoln Street.

He leaned back and watched how the gaggle of girls spoke to one another, so fully engaged, with their eyes continually scanning their opposites, like radar, working to drag more out of each other. He recalled how Cora Lynn would look him over like that. It made him feel like he was being interrogated, as if he weren't doing enough for her. What more did she want from him? Carel sighed loud enough to interrupt the palaver around the table.

"God knows I could never really connect with that woman." Jeanie barged into his thoughts—uncanny how she seemed to know what he was thinking. "Too much makeup, like she was hiding something."

"Well, did you ever get a good look at her complexion? I mean she had a lot to cover up," Gerdie teased.

"That's my wife you're talking about." Carel stopped them. "You might have enough courtesy to carry on this conversation behind my back."

The ladies reached for their glasses in one synchronized motion.

Carel pressed against the back of his chair and distracted himself by rolling his shirt sleeves up in slow, deliberate folds, unable to turn his thoughts away from his wife.

She was suffering right now. Cora Lynn was not one to spaz out or go for the drama, but she was hurt, crushed inside. He had provided the things that he had promised her: the big house, the shiny new truck, and all the status that was going to come with the money they were going to make. Then he pulled it all out from under her. Like none of it was ever real. It would leave a scar on her—he knew that. He had no idea how she would get past that. But it had to be done.

If I lost her with the house, then so be it.

The kitten popped into his face. "My kitty! My kitty, Uncle Carel. He wants some milk."

"Well, you see that man over there?" He pointed across the patio. "His name is Ross."

"The man with the white dress?"

"That's his apron, sweetheart. He won't like it if you call it a dress."

"Okay. Why does he have an apron?"

"You go show him your kitty. He can get you some milk."

Caitlin skipped off on her assigned mission, and Carel turned around to meet the curious stares of a table full of mothers.

"Listen, Carel," his sister said. "Austin could be a good place for you right now. You can come stay with me and Caitlin. This town has had enough of you."

"Thanks for that, sis. But, broke or not, I'm too much a part of this place to end up somewhere else."

"You don't even have a place to stay."

"And no one likes you here," Gerdie threw in, just to taunt him.

Carel smirked back at Gerdie and responded to Jeanie. "I'm going out to Uncle Victor's place. Fix it up. I'm sure the family will let me stay there as long as I make some improvements."

"Uncle Victor's! Why, that place is all broken down." She acted appalled. "No one's lived there since Uncle Victor died. Nothing works out there. No water. No electricity. No nothing."

Carel scooched his chair back to leave. "I figure if a guy's going to start all over again, it's best to start with nothing. That way, you can find out what you really got."

Standing a fair distance from the house, the outside cooker at Uncle Victor's tumbledown ranch was the only thing that wasn't crumbling into decay. Victor Geische and some of his friends had built that cooker when he ranched and rodeoed from his homestead off of Ranger Creek. Seasoned with decades of soot and family memories, the cinderblock trough was the size of a dining room table. It had a tin hood cantilevered with a pail of stones so that it could be lifted open with one hand. Logs of dry oak were burned down to coals on an open fire that was just a shovel toss away from the firebox—a setup that kept a fairly constant temperature for the long, slow smoking that was the defining trait of Geische barbeque.

Carel was using the outside cooker now because the kitchen inside the house didn't have a working stove; it was just hot plates and a microwave oven in there. The icebox was a charming antique that required a particular combination of dry ice and block ice to keep anything cool for longer than a couple of days. The house did have a spigot that ran chalky well water, but that sink was not actually inside the kitchen. The dwelling, a relic of a pioneer home, had figured into Carel's grand plans for the Ranger Creek subdivision. This was the place where the official Texas historical marker was going to go, if he'd ever gotten one. Now he was just trying to put a roof over his own head.

The homestead was family property. With the dreams of a big subdivision—making him the richest Geische of all time—gone bust, the family didn't mind Carel fixing it up so he could do something more practical with the land. Like raise some Spanish goats.

The day that Cora Lynn came back, Carel was sweat-soaked and unshaven. He was on his back, half stuck under the floorboards, trying to fix a saddle clamp onto a rusty old galvanized pipe that had been leaking for at least a dozen years. He could hear the vehicle banging its way up that unpaved caliche road for some time, but he couldn't tell if it was a car or a truck until he heard the door slam shut. He just lay still where he was, hoping that he wouldn't be found.

She stepped carefully across the wary floorboards in high heels and her new hairdo. Sweat stung Carel's eyes as he stared up at her.

"I took that job at Crossing Creek Realty."

"Oh?" Carel wiggled his way out from between the warped planks.

"I had to put a home address on the employment papers. So I just wrote down 'Uncle Victor's old place out on Ranger Creek.' I didn't know if they even had street numbers out here."

"You get street numbers after you get your subdivision permit. We never got that far." Carel shook his head. "And I don't know what's in worse shape, this house or our marriage. What I promised you was a big slice of the pie. I really wanted to make a difference here. I really did. For you and me both. But this is where I ended up. This is all I got for you." With the vice grips still in his hand, he waved his arm around the room. Then sheepishly he added, "Got to build it up from here."

"You mean to say 'all *we* got right now.'" With ladylike grace, Cora Lynn stooped to her heels and leaned over top of him. She spoke softly, as if she were trying to keep a secret from being overheard, her mouth close to his ear. "Ever since I was a little girl, you know, I was planning to marry me a cowboy. Never wanted one of those pantywaist, TV types with the brushed-off hat and the shiny boots and all. But a real tough-guy cowboy with mud on his boots, who might even throw a punch every now and again. I think I got me the real thing here."

She paused, looked back down on him, and said, "Just my luck, damn it." She pressed her cherry red lipstick hard into his stubbled cheek. Carel rolled his dry lips onto hers, and his whole world fell into place.

• • •

On Sunday afternoon Carel had some jalapeño wrapped around a tiny quail breast with a strip of bacon stacked up in Uncle Victor's cooker, next to seven pounds of juice-dripping pork butt. Off to the side he kept a pail of ice with a few longnecks of Lone Star sticking out. Up by the house, a picnic table was crowded with serving bowls covered in aluminum foil: German potato salad, pole beans, sauerkraut.

Half a dozen cousins, Cora Lynn's boys, and some friends had come out to help him shore up the old ranch house—just the kind of thing that the old Germans did around here. Justin and Jordan had brought out a truckload of lumber that they had scavenged from a building site as well as a whole lot of shingles bought on local handshake credit.

Jock Ritzi, the cousin who was no good with a hammer, was banging away on the new roof beams. He stopped from time to time to holler at his kids, who were running through the dilapidated barn. "You boys! You boys stay out of there, or you're going to get your head cut in."

Carel looked over the scene from his spot by the cooker and made a mental note to check the square of that frame where Jock was hammering. He raised the lid to poke at the pork butt and push at the quail wraps.

"You keep that lid down, boy. You know that if you're lookin', you ain't cookin'," said Sheriff Otto, swaggering down the slight decline to the cooker, minding his balance.

"Brought y'all some bread from Mr. Dietz. You can't have a legal picnic in Gillespie County without Dietz's pumpernickel bread."

Carel pulled a Lone Star from an ice pail, popped the top off, and handed it to Otto, all with one hand. The two of them kicked back and watched Jock's son Josh bend down an old fence post and fall to the other side.

"Josh! You get your rump off that fence right now," Jock was hollering from the roof beams. Everyone could hear him, but no one figured that he would come off that ladder. "You get over here right now." Jock's other boys scampered behind the barn, out of earshot.

"Funny how life just goes 'round in circles." Otto gestured with his beer. "Just like you kids back then."

"Which kids?" Carel asked.

"All y'all." Otto looked out over the place he knew so well. "It would all look just like this. We were out there putting up that barn for the first time. That same barn right there. Victor would be standing right there where you are, smokin' a brisket and sucking down a beer. The ladies'd be dressing the table, just like they are now. And you would be running off with *kleiner* Max and old Teddy Hilss's little girl, Mari."

That was enough of a stroll down memory lane for Carel, but he didn't say anything to interrupt the sheriff.

"All three of y'all. You'd be cutting up. Always into something. And you, Carel, you were always the one who got caught with your britches down."

Carel preferred to forget all that.

"That's 'cause you were always tryin' to get ahead of yourself." Otto gave his nephew a slap on the back. "You should be proud that you gave it a good try, Carel. But this here land don't let a boy get too far ahead of himself."

That was the bitter side of this German Hill Country legacy, and Carel knew it well. Everyone gets held in their place.

"We're so blessed to be able to live in a place like Gillespie County," Otto said. "It's good that things don't never change around here."

"Amen to that."

Their bottles clinked together, and they chugged down their beers.

• • •

Willow wasn't moving in with her fiancé like she had told her mom. She kept that secret even as they spent a weekend together sorting through the furniture, closets, and clothes bins deciding what they were going to keep and what they would be giving to St. Vincent de Paul.

"The bank's been calling me. Carel's been calling me too. I'm not answering. They've done enough damage," Mari told her daughter as they lugged a bookshelf off the porch. It was sweaty work, and they both knew this would be the last time they would be doing something together at this house. So they lingered and took a lot of iced-tea breaks out on the front porch.

"Actually think I'll like livin' in the Sunday house." Mari smiled. "It's small and manageable. The first building my family put up on this place. Getting back to my roots."

"There won't be any more bed-and-breakfast money coming in now that you'll be living there."

"I didn't mind the visitors from time to time, but I really didn't care for cleaning up after 'em all the time."

"You worried about the money?"

"I'm always worried about money."

"You can turn it into a whorehouse."

"Willow Geische!" Mari tried to scold while her daughter laughed. "That is the kind of thing a good mother would have taught her daughter never to say."

Willow dug deeper. "The way this town is changing, you never know what's gonna be the next trend."

Mari sighed and took a long drink from her iced tea. When Willow stopped smart-alecking, Mari removed the small silver cross from around her neck, the cross that Willow had so often borrowed. She raised it over her head and placed it around her daughter's neck.

"I'm done now," Mari said without sentiment or a tear. "I gave you all my love. Did all I could as a mother to you. You are in God's hands now."

Willow held off leaving until Sunday evening, when her mother stayed after church for the weekly fellowship dinner—a solid alibi. Willow came by the house alone and tossed the last of her stuff into the black Dodge Challenger that used to belong to one of her fathers.

There was a message from her mother on her phone, but Willow was done with news from her old life. She didn't want anything to weaken her resolve, so she dropped her phone into the downstairs toilet and was done with it. *I'm not coming back.*

Driven by an impulse—the same undoubting urge that had guided razor blades through her skin—Willow started gathering up newspapers and cardboard, she piled them up on the floor next to the stairwell and lit a match under them. She piled on larger pieces of wood—chair legs and kitchen drawers that she had pulled out and busted up into smaller pieces.

Fledgling flames grabbed at the paper, licked at the baseboards, and filled the room with white smoke. After dumping some books on top of the struggling fire. Willow realized this was going to be more of a chore than she had time for. She scuffled out of the house and crossed the yard to the garden shed, where they kept fuel cans for their lawnmower.

If anyone was paying attention, they would have been able to see the windows leaking white smoke. It burned Willow's eyes when she went back in. She couldn't get close to the flames that were scrubbing the lower walls, so she just threw the entire can onto the heap.

A great ball of orange-red flame roared through the room, pushing her backwards and singeing her eyebrows. *That should do it.* Willow felt the air drawing through the kitchen door as she walked out for the last time, deliberately leaving it open and getting into her car.

There was no need for headlights until she was a long way beyond the city limits, past the sign that welcomed visitors with its prophetic greeting:

Fredericksburg

An Enduring Heritage

She was just minutes down the road, and all of that "enduring heritage" was light-years behind her. Past Harper, the next town out, and barely out of Gillespie County, she was starting to get a little antsy behind the wheel. She didn't hear any sirens. No one chasing after her.

Coming upon the big merge onto Interstate 10 in Junction, Texas, Willow was out of the gate, dropping into a slot on the interstate, slipping into the current of fast-moving cars and trucks, with the fading light of the Hill Country framed in the back window like the disappearing image on a postcard. The speed of the Challenger crept up of its own volition. The familiar radio stations crackled off the air, and a slow darkness rolled onto the highway until her entire world lay in the narrow cones of her own headlights. Road signs went past in a blur . . .

Sonora	28 mi
Ozona	62 mi
El Paso	624 mi

. . . with nothing in between. Five more hours of driving, and she would still be a long way from the Texas border—a long way to the rest of her life.

KHOS 92.1, the old country music station out of Sonora, was all Willow could find on the far side of the hills. She took it on board like a hitchhiker, something that she didn't like but that would keep her company until, hours later, it got lost in a puddle of static. Then there was nothing but that endless spackle of stars and the occasional QuickStop with its dirty bathrooms and stale iced tea. Crossing through a West Texas night was like shooting through a rabbit hole, some kind of bend in reality that needs to be breached before you can get beyond the long reach of the ones who claim they love you. Willow figured it was a drive best done at night, when the highway was cool and the anguished desolation of the Permian Basin was hidden in the dark.

Well behind her, an orange and yellow blaze licked at the walls of her past like the flames of a baptism reaching out to wash her clean. If there was some kind of mission to all of this, Willow didn't know what it was. She didn't care. She was just driving.

ABOUT THE AUTHOR

MARC HESS has lived in Fredericksburg long enough to see this venerable and rock-rimmed German farming community morph into the chic, new-age tourist destination that it is today. Steeped in a career of magazine publishing and travel writing, Marc is the founding publisher of *The Insider's Guide To The Texas Hills* and has raised his family among the Germans who cling tightly to the beauty of their heritage. Marc currently serves on the Board of Directors of the Writer's League of Texas.